The Summer the Air Changed

PADGETT GERLER

Jan-Carol
Publishing, Inc

"every story needs a book"

The Summer the Air Changed
Padgett Gerler

Published July 2021
Little Creek Books
Imprint of Jan-Carol Publishing, Inc.
All rights reserved
Copyright © 2021

ISBN: 978-1-954978-05-8
Library of Congress Control Number: 2021937487

You may contact the publisher:
Jan-Carol Publishing, Inc.
PO Box 701
Johnson City, TN 37605
publisher@jancarolpublishing.com
www.jancarolpublishing.com

Dedicated to

Susan Sponaugle,

the sister of my heart,

whose love and support softened the sharp edges of 2020,

and whose friendship continues to comfort me.

ONE

Bug Jeter and
the Jesus Rock

I guess you might say it all started that day Bug Jeter seen Jesus in a rock.

Me and my best friend, Wisteria, were sitting at the lunch counter in my Uncle Ted's drugstore, minding our own business—which, as Mama says, is a rarity, since me and Wisteria are known for insinuating ourselves into other folks' affairs. Wisteria started swiveling back and forth and twirling on her red vinyl stool, something that drives me crazy.

"You're gonna have to cut out that swiveling and twirling if you want to stay my best friend. You already know from past twirlings that that is gonna flat-out drive me crazy in just a couple of minutes."

"I believe our best-friend contract says you have to put up with my twirling," Wisteria said, without slowing down even a little bit.

Our contract—and, yes, we do have a best-friend contract, thanks to Wisteria—doesn't say any such thing. But every time I take exception to something Wisteria is doing or saying, she tells me she's pretty sure whatever it is is in our best-friend contract.

But she said she couldn't sit still because of her nervous energy.

1

"It's either swivel or tap dance, and I don't believe your Uncle Ted would take too kindly to me entertaining his customers with my tap dancing."

"What you got nervous energy for this time?"

"Don't know, Bit, but something's in the air. I can feel it in my bones. It's making my hair follicles itch."

"Well, you can tap dance later, but for the time being, just sit still." Once I got her slowed down, I said, "Selma, could you please fix us two extra-large Cherry Co-Colas?"

"Sure thing, sweetie," Selma said.

Even though Selma knows everybody's name in Lovington and surrounding areas, she calls all of us sweetie. Except Uncle Ted. My Uncle Ted's her boss, so she calls him Ted. Not sweetie.

As she was fixing our Cherry Co-Colas, Uncle Ted yelled across from the pharmacy where he was counting out pills, "On the house, Selma."

"Sure thing, Ted," Selma said and gave us one of her most congenial winks.

Then me and Wisteria turned around, Wisteria spinning a couple extra times for good measure, and we both called out, "Thanks, Uncle Ted. We owe you one."

We actually owed Uncle Ted many because he never made me and Wisteria pay for our extra-large Cherry Co-Colas.

Selma plunked down our glasses on the counter and stabbed each of them with a straw. Wisteria had finally halted her spinning and was just swinging her legs back and forth, kicking the counter in front of her, making Selma's congenial winks turn into slitty-eye stares. So we were slurping and Wisteria was kicking away when Miss Novelle Fairchild came screeching in the drugstore, wearing her apron over her housedress and waving her pudgy hands all frantic-like.

"Ted, Ted, you gotta come right now!"

Whenever anything happens in Lovington, North Carolina, whether it be good news or sad news or wacky news, the news teller comes running to my Uncle Ted first. He may be younger than my daddy, but even Daddy says he's the smartest one of the Sizemore brothers. He and Daddy and Uncle Double are all on the town council, but Uncle Ted is the president. He has been ever since he came back home after graduating from pharmacy school over at the University, married Aunt Sally, and opened Sizemore Drugs down on Main Street.

Anyway, Miss Novelle came in the drugstore, screeching for my Uncle Ted.

He rushed from behind the pharmacy counter, took Miss Novelle's hand, and patted it. "Now, calm down, Miss Novelle. You're going to cause yourself to faint again. And Doc Spivey just took the stitches out of your chin from your last spell. Come on over here and sit down at the lunch counter." He turned to Selma and said, "Selma, fix Miss Novelle a Co-Cola, will you, please?"

Once he had Miss Novelle settled down and sipping her Co-Cola, Uncle Ted said, "Now, Miss Novelle, tell me real slow what's going on that shook you up so bad."

She dabbed her eyes with her frilly apron hem and said, "Bug Jeter, that crazy old coot, said he seen Jesus in a rock! Well, you know how he gets when he starts to hittin' the bottle, so I didn't believe a word he was saying. But just to humor him and get him off my front porch—'cause, you know, I don't want the neighbors thinking I'm *keeping company* with that old fool—I told him I'd go take a look. I was in the middle of making an apple crumb pie for Cora June, 'cause you know her daddy just passed here Thursday was a week ago, and I didn't even stop to take off my apron or dust the flour off my hands since I figured I'd be right back. Well, the rock in question was just down the holler road a spell from my house, so I toddled on down there, trailing that crazy Bug. When we finally got there, Bug stabbed his finger toward that rock and said, 'See there? Told ya so.' Well, I couldn't believe my eyes. Lord have mercy, Ted, that old fool was telling the truth! There really is a likeness of Jesus on a big old rock, sitting right there 'side the holler road."

Of course, since me and Wisteria were sitting right there at the counter, we heard every last word Miss Novelle said about Bug seeing Jesus in a rock. And this time we didn't even have to eavesdrop, what with all her screeching and carrying on so.

"Let's go see," said Wisteria.

"Well, of course," I said back, like there was any question at all about me and Wisteria staying out of it.

"Selma," I said, "will you watch our Cherry Co-Colas till me and Wisteria get back from seeing Bug's Jesus rock?

"Have you taken leave of your senses, Bit Sizemore?" Selma asked, not calling me sweetie this one time. She raised her Revlon #19 Charcoal eyebrows at me and yanked off her ruffled apron with the pink cabbage roses, tossing it on the prep table. Already heading for the door, she called back over her shoulder, "I ain't staying here to guard your Cherry Co-Colas. I'm gonna go see that Jesus rock for myself."

When she got to the door, she yelled over at my Uncle Ted, "Ted, I may be back, but, then again, maybe I won't. Depends on how transformative Bug's Jesus rock proves to be."

"Okay, Selma," Uncle Ted called back, not even looking up from tending to Miss Novelle. "You do what you have to do."

Uncle Ted wasn't at all worried. Selma always came back. That's because Selma had been with my Uncle Ted since the day he opened Sizemore Drugs down on Main Street in Lovington, North Carolina. Me and Buddy were helping Uncle Ted sweep up and dust and stock the shelves before he opened his door for business when Selma strolled in, looked around, and sort of hired herself on.

"Ted Sizemore, looks like you're gonna need some help around here."

"Probably will, Miss Selma. You come to help me?"

"That I have, Ted. I've known you since you was knee-high. Knew way back then you was gonna make something big of yourself. As usual, I was right," she said, laughing her big old raspy laugh and pushing her Clairol-yellow curls out of her eyes. "But, son, you can't run this whole thing all by yourself."

"True, true, Miss Selma. What do you plan to do to help me out?"

"Well, Ted, I figure you can take care of the pills, and I'll take full charge of the lunch counter. Cooking, cleaning, ordering—the whole kit 'n caboodle."

"That sounds like a good deal, Miss Selma. How much will your services set me back?"

"Oh, Ted, let's not quibble over numbers right now. We'll settle all that later."

Uncle Ted agreed with Selma's arrangement, knowing full well she'd be reasonable. But he drew the line at calling his business Selma and Sizemore.

And, just like that, Selma more or less hired herself on to run the lunch counter at Sizemore Drugs, and Uncle Ted hadn't even placed an ad for employment. Also, just like that, Selma and my Uncle Ted became two of the most unlikely best friends in all of Lovington, North Carolina.

Except for maybe me and my best friend, Wisteria.

TWO

Wisteria Calliope Jones Submits Her Application for Friendship

It wasn't too long before Bug Jeter seen Jesus in the rock that Naomi June Lockleer had to move to Weaverton when her daddy got that forklift-operating job over at the paper mill. I'd been pouting and feeling sorry for myself, seeing as how my best friend was gone and all, but nobody paid any attention or joined in to feeling sorry for me. So I flopped from chair to chair, sighing real pitiful-like, but still Mama and Daddy and Buddy went on about their business like nothing tragic had even happened.

Then there came a knock on the front door.

Mama yelled from the kitchen, "Bit, I'm elbow deep in flour. Could you please quit your sighing long enough to see who's at the door?"

I stopped watching cartoons, which is something else I'd done a whole lot of while I flopped from chair to chair since Naomi June Lockleer had moved over to Weaverton and left me without a best friend. I shuffled all heavy-like over to the front door. When I opened it, I saw this funny-looking kid standing there. She was smiling real big, and I noticed right away she had a great big gap between her two front teeth.

She was short, about three inches shorter than me, but back then, before I had my growth spurt, I was pretty short myself. She had bright-orange hair pulled back tight into French braids that hung way down her back. She had a face full of orange freckles that matched her hair exactly, and she wore little gold-rimmed glasses that rode way down on her nose. The lenses of her glasses were so smudged and grimy, I found it hard to believe that she could even see through them.

She pushed her glasses back up to where they were supposed to be and squinched up her pale blue eyes at me. She whistled through that gap in her teeth when she said, "Hi, my name is Wisteria Calliope Jones, and it has come to my attention that your best friend, Naomi June Lockleer, has recently moved over to Weaverton, leaving you best friendless. Coincidentally, I find myself best friendless at this time, as well, as I have just moved to the holler with my mama and daddy, Faylene and Daddy Earl, and my brothers, Luke and Earl, Jr., and my little sisters, Faye and Virginia.

"We're living down by the river in a rickety little trailer my grand-daddy Papa Luke owns until Daddy Earl can build a respectable three-bedroom, one-and-one-half bath, brick ranch-style home for us to live in. Daddy Earl was recently hired on as a supervisor at Enoch Murtry's Construction Company over by the bypass, so he knows how to build houses real good."

When she stopped to take a breath, I jumped in and said, "Hey, Wisteria." And since she had told me all about her family, I thought maybe I was supposed to tell her all about mine. It was something I wasn't accustomed to doing, but I figured I could use the practice. "I'm Bit Sizemore. I been living here in this house in the holler all my life with my mama and daddy, Brenda and Harrison, and my big brother, Buddy. Mama's a stay-at-home mama, but my daddy and my Uncle Double own Sizemore Electric and Plumbing Company right off River Road down in Lovington. Buddy's two years older 'n me, and he goes to Lovington High School. Sometimes he works after school and on weekends with Daddy down at Sizemore Electric and Plumbing Company. Me, I'm not old enough to work. I'm just a stay-at-home kid. But during the week I do go to Lovington Middle School."

She grabbed my hand and pumped it real hard and fast. "I know all about you already. I would not have come a'calling today without first doing my research. The real reason I am here is I would like to apply for the position to be your best friend, since we both find ourselves best friendless at this time. That is unless the position has already been filled and unless me living in Papa Luke's rickety little trailer down by the river, even though it is a temporary arrangement, would make a difference in your decision."

Since I didn't have any other best-friend requests at the time and since her living in her Papa Luke's rickety little trailer down by the river didn't make me any nevermind, I said, "Well, I guess you better come on in the house where we can talk about it."

When I said that she'd better come on in the house, she charged right past me into the living room, hopped up on the sofa, and started banging the toes of her orange high-top tennis shoes together, in time to her talking.

"I see you've been watching cartoons," she said. "That's good. That means we have that in common. I like cartoons very much."

"Good, I'm glad you do," I told her.

"Now that I'm looking up close, I see that me and you have freckles in common too," she said.

"Yeah, my mama said if I didn't put on a hat when I went out in the sun, I was gonna get all freckly. She was right."

"Well," Wisteria said, "mine didn't have a dang thing to do with the sun. I was just born this way. But I can see that our resemblance stops at the freckles. I kinda prefer my orange hair, but your curly, sorta-blonde hair is quite becoming. And your brown eyes are lovely."

"Thanks for the compliments. Me and Buddy got our brown eyes and sorta-blonde hair from our mama. We don't look like our daddy a'tall since he has green eyes and black hair. He told Mama he thinks the mailman brought us." Then I told Wisteria, "I really like your orange hair. It not only matches your freckles, it also matches your shoes."

"That is true," she said. "Buying these shoes was no accident. I got them 'cause they match my hair."

Then she cleared her throat and looked seriously over the top of her smudged glasses. "Now, Bit, this is why I would like to be best friends with you. I am new down at the school, and I've been checking out all the girls in my class to see if they would make good best friends. They all seem right nice, but none of them look to me to be best-friend material."

She took a deep breath and went on. "Then I saw you playing that piano up there on the stage at assembly last Friday, and I said to myself, *Wisteria Calliope Jones, that Bit Sizemore's got gumption to sit up there on that stage in front of all these people, playing that piano.* And, Bit, I like gumption in a girl. Gumption makes good best-friend material."

"Thank you, Wisteria. Do you have gumption?" I asked her, not real sure what gumption was.

"Why, yes, I do. That's why I believe me and you would make a good team. But I bring lots more than gumption to this friendship," she said.

Then she reached into her pocket and pulled out a crumpled sheet of blue lined paper. Unfolding it and smoothing it out on her leg, which sported a big scab that I could see through the hole in the knee of her overalls, she cleared her throat and started reading.

"Things that I, Wisteria Calliope Jones, bring to a friendship... Number one: I am very funny. I promise to have at least one new joke to tell you each time we meet. For example, what did the paper say to the pencil?"

She waited for me to answer, but when I gave up, shrugged, and said, "I don't know," she screamed, "Write on!

"See? Funny, huh?"

When I laughed and told her I thought it was real funny, she said, "Well, there's lots more where that one came from."

"Number two: I am a very good swimmer. I recently received my Certificate of Satisfactory Completion from the Pollywog swimming class at the Moorestown YMCA. Of course, I'd already received my Certificate of Satisfactory Completion from the Tadpole swimming class. You can't be a Pollywog if you ain't already been a Tadpole."

"That's very good, Wisteria. I like swimming too."

"Yes, I know that. Like I told you, I've done my research."

I was starting to feel like Wisteria had been following me around, spying on me. Even if she had, though, I just couldn't help but like her. I was already thinking she'd make pretty good best-friend material.

"Number three: I can shoot a gun good as any stupid old boy. Fact is, I can shoot *better* than most, even my brother Luke. And he's pretty good, but don't tell him I said so. I own my very own twenty-two, and I can hit a squirrel right 'tween the eyes, depending on how far away it is, of course. And I can skin that sucker with one hand," she said, snapping her wrist real fast, like she was showing me how. "Right impressive, huh?"

"Yeah, *real* impressive," I told her.

"But I don't believe in shooting a gun just willy-nilly," she said very seriously, with her eyebrows all scrunched up. "They're dangerous equipment and not to be trifled with."

I told Wisteria that I agreed with her about that.

"Now, I'll use my gun for target practice and for shooting squirrels and rabbits—you know, stuff to feed the family—but I'd never go around shooting at animals just for the sport of it."

"That makes good sense."

"Well, just so you understand, Bit. I'm a very responsible gun owner."

"Sure, I understand, but, just so you know, I can't shoot a gun at all."

"That's okay. I'm sure you'll bring other talents to our friendship, like playing the piano. I don't play the piano. So you do all the piano playing, and I'll do all the shooting, but only when it's necessary."

"Sounds good," I said.

"And speaking of shooting squirrels, my mama, Faylene, cooks up my squirrel with cream gravy and puts it on rice. Yum. That's my favorite. Next time Mama cooks squirrel with cream gravy, I'll ask her if you can come for supper. Course, it'll have to be after we move into our respectable three-bedroom, one-and-one-half bath, brick ranch-style house 'cause there's hardly enough room in the rickety little trailer down by the river for the seven of us Joneses."

"Thanks, Wisteria. I'd like that," I told her.

"Yeah, I figured you would," she said.

"Number four: I dance pretty good. Well, I'm very good at tap dancing. My teacher says I have lots of nervous energy and that it comes out through my feet when I tap dance. I'm not too good at ballet, though. I think it is very hard to be good at something you don't like, and I don't like ballet because it makes me look like a damn sissy, and I hate damn sissies. Now, I didn't really say damn sissy. My granddaddy Papa Luke said I looked like a damn sissy when I wore a tutu and did ballet. So I'm not really cussin'. I'm just quotin' my Papa Luke."

I had to pinch my lips together to keep from busting out laughing, and I was hoping my mama couldn't hear Wisteria cussing from the kitchen.

"Number five: I am very smart. That is another thing I think we have in common. My research tells me that you are a very smart person too."

"Well, yeah, I'm pretty smart. Or so my teachers say."

Without remarking on me agreeing with her that I was smart, she went on, "I taught myself to read when I was just three years old. I'm sure you have noticed that I have a better-than-average vocabulary for a person my age, which, by the way, is twelve and one-eighth years old. My IQ has been tested and appears to be way above average. My teachers have shown their astonishment."

I could hardly keep from laughing out loud. I'd never heard a kid talk about her IQ and about teachers being astonished at her brilliance. But I just kept my lips pinched to keep from laughing at her, and Wisteria went on talking.

"I realize that you are already fourteen years old and are in the ninth grade, but I am only one grade behind you. That is because when I went to kindergarten, I could already say and write my alphabet and say and write my numbers all the way to the number twenty. And I had already read the entire first-grade primer and all the Golden Books at the Piggly Wiggly check-out since I had been reading for several years. Guess they figured it didn't make sense to keep me in kindergarten to play sandbox and Play Dough when I could already read and write and count good as a first grader. So they skipped me right over and plunked me down in first grade. Didn't seem to hurt me none. I ain't never made less than an A."

"Being very smart is a good quality to have if you are planning to be best friends with an older girl," I told her.

"Yes, I agree," she said, nodding her head, real matter of fact.

"Number six: I am a very loyal friend. If you choose me as your best friend, I promise that I will be your best friend for as long as you want me to be."

I said, "That's the best quality of all. I'm glad you have that one."

"So am I, Bit," Wisteria said, still whistling through the big old gap in her front teeth.

"Now, do you have any questions you'd like to ask me? Anything I've forgotten?"

"Well, Wisteria, I believe you've just about covered all the fine points for being a best friend."

"All right, then, I'll leave you alone to think about your decision. Just curious, though, how good do you suppose my chances are?"

"I believe your chances are very good, Wisteria. In fact, I think you're the front-runner."

"I was hoping you'd say that. How long do you think it will take you to make your best-friend choice?

"Well, Wisteria, you're in luck 'cause I believe I can make that choice right now."

Balling her fists and pressing them into her thighs, she stretched her mouth into a wide grin, making her lips real skinny, took a deep breath, and said, "Okay, give it to me straight. I can take it."

So I said, "Wisteria, I would be honored if you would be my new best friend."

Since she seemed to have her heart set on being my best friend, I expected her to jump up and whoop with glee. But she didn't. Instead, she reached into her pocket and pulled out two more crumpled sheets of blue, lined paper, unfolded them, and said, "I was hoping that would be your decision, so I have drawn up a best-friend contract and a list of activities we can start with."

Holding up my hand in a sort of stop sign, I said, "Wisteria, I'll sign your best-friend contract, if that's part of the deal, but let's not follow a list. Let's just be friends and see what happens, okay?"

Looking kind of hurt, she refolded her papers real careful-like and slipped them back in her pocket. "Well, I'll hold onto my list, just in case we start to meander," Wisteria said, patting her pocket.

Taking Wisteria's hand and moseying on in the kitchen, I said, "Mama, I got me a new best friend."

Without looking up from crimping the edge of her pie shell, Mama blew a long wisp of her sorta-blonde hair out of her eyes and said, "Well, good, Bit. I was getting awful weary of your heavy sighing."

"Mama, this is Wisteria Calliope Jones, Mr. Luke Jones's granddaughter."

"Well, hi there, Wisteria, nice to meet you," Mama said, still concentrating on her pie shell.

"And it's a pleasure to meet you, too, Miss Brenda. And pardon my forwardness, but is it okay for me to call you Miss Brenda?"

"Of course, Wisteria, Miss Brenda will be fine," Mama said, looking up from her pie making just long enough to give me a wink.

"Come on, Wisteria, let's go on up to the pond and start being best friends."

"Good idea," she said, trudging after me out the back door and up the path through the woods to the pond.

When we reached the pond, I saw that the dock had gotten pretty worn and warped. Our daddies were gonna have to get up there and replace all those bent or rotted boards and nail down all the loose ones so nobody could stub a toe or get a splinter or trip and fall.

Wisteria stepped up onto the dock and started walking real careful, heel-toe, heel-toe, with her arms stretched out from her sides, like she was walking a tightrope and might fall over into the water if she wasn't real cautious. Well, she made it safely out to the end of the dock and sat down and dangled her feet over the edge. Her legs were so short that her feet were several inches from touching the water. I sat down cross-legged beside her and noticed that the air coming off the pond was a mite chilly, so I wrapped my jacket around me tight and tucked my bare hands under my armpits.

Then Wisteria took a real deep breath, and, without looking at me, she said, "Bit, I can only be your six-days-a-week best friend. I can be your best friend Monday through Saturday, but I can't be your best friend on Sunday."

"And why is that?" I asked her.

"'Cause you're a Piscopalian."

"What's wrong with Episcopalians?"

"Well, we's Bible-thumping Baptists, or so my Papa Luke calls us, and Mama and Daddy Earl said that Piscopalians drink the devil's brew right in church and that we can't be associating with that kind of behavior on the Lord's day. But I think Mama and Daddy Earl are calling the kettle black 'cause Papa Luke makes moonshine in the woods right up 'hind his house. But I guess that don't matter none since Papa Luke ain't nothin'—Christianwise, that is. But after meeting your mama, I'm not sure I can believe what Mama and Daddy Earl say about Piscopalians. Miss Brenda is pretty and smells like peanut butter and Jergens lotion. I can't imagine anybody pretty who smells like peanut butter and Jergens lotion drinking the devil's brew. But even if that is true, like Mama and Daddy Earl say it is, if you have one of them potluck suppers on the church grounds on, say, a Wednesday night and there ain't no wine drinking, I believe I could be coaxed to attend with you."

"Okay, I'll remember that," I said.

Then, out of the blue, Wisteria asked, "Want to know why my name is Wisteria Calliope Jones?"

"Sure," I said, because I really was curious about how a little girl got such a fancy name as Wisteria Calliope Jones.

"Well, Mama said if she was gonna get stuck with a boring last name like Jones, she had every right to give her young'un other names that were melodious. And she said that even though she is a mountain girl at heart, she believes her soul was born in Charleston, South Carolina. She said that Wisteria Calliope sounded like somebody who would live in Charleston. And she said that Wisteria Calliope also sounded quite melodious.

"Now, Mama named my brothers Luke after Papa Luke and Earl, Jr. after Daddy Earl. Then she called my little sister Faye after herself, herself being named Faylene Brackett Jones. When she named my babiest sister Virginia, I said, 'Mama, if your soul was born in Charleston, how come you didn't name your babiest girl South Carolina, instead of Virginia?' Mama thought that was so funny, and you know how I like being funny, so I said it over and over and over till Mama said to hush because it had ceased to be amusing after the forty-zillionth time."

I laughed 'cause that really was funny.

"See there? I promised you a joke each visit."

"That's right, you did."

"Okay, now that you know how I got my name, tell me how you come to be called Bit. I couldn't find that tidbit of information in my research."

"Well, soon as I was born, Buddy—who was only about two years old at the time—held out his arms and said, 'My baby, hold my baby.'"

Mama told him, "'Buddy, you gotta be careful 'cause she's just an itty-bitty baby. So Buddy started calling me Itty Bitty Baby. Guess that got to be too much of a mouthful, so he just shortened it to Bit. But every once in a while, he'll call me Itty Bitty. I kinda like it when he does that. Now, my given name is Mary Margaret, after both my grandmas, but people have always just called me Bit."

"Interesting story. I like interesting stories. I'm sure you'll bring many interesting stories to our friendship."

"I'll try," I said.

Then Wisteria got distracted by the hole in her overalls and noticed the scab on her knee. And she started picking at it.

Without looking at me she said, "Now that we're best friends, I can tell you the real reason we moved to Lovington."

"Why's that, Wisteria?"

"My mama said Daddy Earl was up to no good, and she said she had to bring us up here so his daddy, that's Papa Luke, could keep an eye on him. And Mama said Daddy Earl would never be up to no good under his daddy's watchful eye."

I noticed her eyes tearing up while she concentrated on picking at the scab on her knee.

She wiped her sleeve across her eyes and said, "I don't cry. Damn sissies cry. And, as you know, I hate damn sissies. And, once again, I ain't cussin'. I'm quotin'."

I didn't know what to say to her since I was just a kid myself and didn't have experience with such things as daddies being up to no good, whatever that meant, so, sounding like my mama, I said, "You better stop worrying with that scab, Wisteria. It'll never heal."

So she stopped picking at her knee...for the time being.

Then she spit in the palm of her hand and looked at me.

When I didn't do anything, she said, "What'cha waiting for? Spit in your hand."

So I spit in the palm of my hand and waited to see what would happen.

Wisteria grabbed my hand, slapped our palms together and screamed real loud, her voice echoing over the pond, "Best friends! Forever!"

THREE

A Town Full of Yella-headed Ladies in Sensible Shoes

Since me and Wisteria signed our best-friend contract, we've had a good number of adventures, but we hadn't ever heard of anything like a Jesus rock.

So we left our Cherry Co-Colas unguarded and took off running out the drugstore. We figured it was worth getting our Cherry Co-Colas stolen to see a Jesus rock. But, then, who'd want two half-drunk Cherry Co-Colas?

Wisteria went streaking toward the holler road, and I was having a hard time keeping up with her. I screamed for her to hold up, but she yelled back over her shoulder that I was well aware that her orange high-tops were magic and that they made her run like the wind. Since I was wearing my plain old white low-tops that made me run just regular, I was out of breath and had a hitch in my side by the time I caught up with her. What's more, we weren't expecting to have to compete for running space with about twenty-five other people already trudging up the road to see Bug's Jesus rock.

Word spreads like crazy around little Lovington, North Carolina.

Wisteria flew past that whole crowd, with me panting after her and grabbing onto that side hitch. When we reached Bug's Jesus rock, there was already a crowd gathered 'round, and me and Wisteria had to squeeze ourselves in between folks till we shimmied our way to the front.

And I'll be dang if Bug wasn't telling the truth, just like Miss Novelle said he was. Right there on that rock was a big old likeness of Jesus, right down to his beard and gentle, forgiving eyes.

Seeing that Jesus likeness on Bug's rock reminded me of the time that man over in Pigeon Forge saw the face of Abraham Lincoln on his pancake down at the Waffle House. He saved that pancake in a plastic baggie, but it got moldy, and Abe's face faded away in about a week. But I figured this rock wasn't gonna get moldy, and I couldn't see Jesus going anywhere any time soon.

Course, Bug took seeing the likeness of Jesus on a rock as some sort of sign from heaven. He laid down his bottle and walked right down to the Baptist church, where Wisteria's family worshipped every Sunday. Every time the doors opened, Bug was right there in the front pew, praising the Lord, waving his hands in the air, and singing louder than everybody else. Before those Baptists knew it, he was right there in the pulpit, spouting scripture and giving his testimonial. Guess when you see Jesus on a rock, an instant believer can leap-frog over lifetime follow-ers right into the pulpit.

Daddy said, "Thank the good Lord Bug decided to become a Baptist. We don't need any more screwball Episcopalians."

It wasn't long before word got out past the holler that Bug Jeter had seen Jesus in a rock. Somebody told somebody who told somebody else, and the story grew clean over to the Capital. And once the story hit the Internet, there were news trucks crawling all over the holler and lady reporters in suits and high heels clomping up and down our gravel road.

It was amazing how hard those reporters worked to make a story out of Bug Jeter and the Jesus rock. They even interviewed Doc Spivey because he was the doctor who had delivered Bug. Once Doc said he'd delivered him, though, he didn't have much else to say about him. The reporters went into Mr. Carl Bumper's diner, but all Mr. Carl could tell them was that Bug came in for a soda every once in a while and that his favorite was Orange Crush. They talked to the Baptist minister, Brother Grady Grantham, who said that Bug was a devout Christian, even though he'd only been one for about seventeen days.

When he heard the reporters were coming to the school that Bug Jeter had attended, Mr. Peoples, our principal, decided to roll out the red carpet. We had a pep rally out on the football field with the cheerleaders and majorettes and marching band performing. When the TV reporters got there, nobody could think of much to say about Bug since he'd dropped out of school in the fifth grade. But it was a big day for our school, seeing as how we were going to be on TV and all. We rushed home that afternoon to watch ourselves on the evening news. Didn't last more than about fifteen seconds, but there we were, me and Wisteria sitting in the front row of the bleachers, clapping our hands and singing our school fight song right along with the marching band.

"Good lord," Daddy said, shaking his head in disbelief, "you'd think Bug had discovered that Virgin Mary statue that cries blood."

Lot of folks must have been watching the news when they reported on Bug's Jesus rock, because pretty soon the holler was crawling with cars full of yella-headed ladies in sensible shoes, all of them asking where they could find The Jesus Rock. Once they had their directions, they'd go whizzing up the holler road, expecting something like

Mount Rushmore, I'm guessing, and ending up being pretty let down by the uneventfulness of it. But once they'd seen The Jesus Rock, which didn't take but about a minute, I'm figuring they decided they'd might as well make a day of it in Lovington since they'd come all that way from wherever they lived. So those ladies would make their way down the holler road into town, where they'd bide their time, eating lunch at Mr. Carl's diner, shopping for clothes at Miss Dixie May's shop, filling up their cars with gas at Mr. Fisher's filling station, buying corn pads and hair spray in Uncle Ted's drugstore. Then they'd mosey on past the Strand Theatre—which was only open for Wednesday and Saturday matinees and one showing on Saturday night—and stop in at Mama and Miss Nelda's quilt shop, which started off more like a social club than a real store.

Before The Quilt Shop opened, Mama and Miss Nelda and all their quilting-club ladies would meet in our living room to do their quilting and gossiping. Daddy would come home from work to find that his supper wasn't on the table, and he couldn't even get to the sofa to watch the evening news.

So he told Mama, "Brenda, you and Nelda find a place other than our living room to do your quilting, and I'll gladly pay the rent. All I ask is that you be here with something for me to eat and no gabbing ladies when I get home from work at night. Deal?"

"Deal," Mama said, and she and Miss Nelda set out to find some place to quilt and gossip, other than in front of Daddy's TV.

Didn't take long for the ladies to move their quilting-and-gossiping operation out of our living room. Miss Nelda's daddy, Mr. Claude Jenkins, owned the old Mercantile Store on Main Street, about halfway between the Strand Theatre and Lovington High School, which is the same school as Lovington Elementary School and Lovington Middle School. Lovington Elementary School is on the first floor, Lovington Middle School is on the middle floor, which I think is very convenient, and Lovington High School is on the top floor. But when anyone talks about the school, they just call it Lovington High School.

Anyway, Mr. Jenkins ran the old Mercantile Store until he closed it some years back, when the Walmart went in over by the bypass and took most of his business away. But Mr. Jenkins said that was fine, because he was getting good and tired of inventorying lipstick and whatnot, and he was ready to retire anyway. So now he spends his summers fly fishing in the river down below his house in the holler and winters playing bocce ball and eating seafood down in Boca Raton, Florida.

The building had just been sitting there empty, gathering dust and breeding mice nests and being a regular eyesore. Old Mr. Jenkins said that the ladies could use the building, rent free, to quilt and gossip and do whatever else they wanted to do, just as long as it wasn't illegal or immoral. All they'd have to do was clean it up and pay to have the electricity and water turned back on.

"It might work, Nelda," Mama said. "When can we take a look?"

"I've got the key," Miss Nelda said, pulling it out of her pocket.

So Mama and Miss Nelda looked it over, sidestepping the mice nests, and said it had good bones, with wooden floors and lots of room to spread out their quilts. Everybody, including Daddy and Miss Nelda's husband, Mr. Fred, their four kids and Buddy and me, pitched in to get the building presentable. I believe Daddy would have agreed to anything to have his living room, his TV, and his supper back.

Then Mama said, "Nelda, while we're at it, why don't we open a quilt store here. We already have the old cash register and glass cases and shelves from your daddy's mercantile store. Who knows, maybe we'll sell a quilt every now and then to the folks who come up to look at the fall leaves and wander around town looking for a souvenir of their trip."

Miss Nelda thought that sounded like a good idea, so once the two of them had gone over to the county seat to get all the licenses and whatever else they'd need to start a store, they opened their doors for business—but mostly for quilting and gossiping.

Then Bug Jeter seen Jesus in a rock, and the yella-headed ladies in sensible shoes found out about it.

Turns out yella-headed ladies in sensible shoes *love* hand-made quilts, leastwise the ones who came to see The Jesus Rock did. They'd buy a quilt from The Quilt Shop and take it on back home, wherever home might be, and show some other yella-headed ladies. Then *those* yella-headed ladies would come to see The Jesus Rock and stop by The Quilt Shop to make a purchase. Then they'd go home and tell their friends and so on and so forth. As our math teacher, Mr. Nicely, would say, the quilting business grew exponentially.

Fact is, everything in Lovington grew exponentially.

"I just wanted a family pharmacy," my Uncle Ted said, "one that would cater to all the people I love, all the people who have been so supportive of me all my life. I never dreamed I'd be working nights to place extra orders for aspirin and corn pads and feminine products. And I've had to run an ad in the Gazette for a second fry cook to handle all the extra grilled cheese sandwiches and hot dogs on the lunch shift. Selma can't take care of it all by herself anymore. Mind you, I appreciate the extra business, but I just wasn't expecting it. So I wasn't prepared."

Neither was Mr. Carl down at the diner. He had to put more tables inside the restaurant until they were almost slam up against one another, and he'd even set tables and chairs out on the sidewalk for the overflow. He called the sidewalk tables and chairs a bistro, like they have in Paris, France. Wisteria called it eating lunch on the sidewalk on Main Street. But the yella-headed ladies seemed to love standing in line to eat at the sidewalk bistro outside Mr. Carl's diner.

Mr. Fisher down at the filling station ran out of gas by Wednesday that week Bug Jeter seen Jesus in a rock. He had to call his gas delivery man and tell him that he was gonna have to start coming every week to fill his tank, instead of every two weeks. Even with his weekly deliveries, before long he was pumping fumes by the end of the week. But Mr. Fisher wasn't complaining. He liked the extra business. And he liked the ladies. He'd get to talking to them, cleaning their windows, checking the air in their tires, because, unlike the big-city gas stations where people had to pump their own gas, Mr. Fisher had a full-service gas station. And while he worked, he'd wink at those ladies and flatter them and make them giggle.

He'd smile real big, puff out his chest, and say, "I send 'em away satisfied."

Miss Dixie had so many shoppers looking for casual clothes that she had to put in two new rounders of corduroy trousers and quilted jackets and turtleneck sweaters, along with a couple shelves of comfortable walking shoes.

Then one day Miss Eulalee Pinckney came running into Uncle Ted's drugstore all excited because, like I said, whenever anybody's got any excitement or whatever to share, they take it to Uncle Ted's.

Once again, Wisteria and I were at Uncle Ted's lunch counter. We were eating grilled cheese sandwiches with dill pickles and drinking Cherry Co-Colas, and Wisteria was, as usual, swiveling back and forth on her stool.

That's when we heard Miss Eulalee bellow, "Glory be, it came to me in a vision!"

We looked up, all astonished, to see her smiling real big and holding a lavender lace hanky against her great big old pillow bosoms.

Miss Eulalee was an elderly spinster lady with curly blue hair. Since her mama and daddy had passed a good ten years back, she had rattled around all by herself in that big old eight-bedroom Victorian house with the twelve-foot-high ceilings down there on Main Street between Doc Spivey's house and the Piggly Wiggly.

"I am going to turn the old homeplace into a B&B." Looking around the drugstore to make sure everybody was listening to her plan, she said, "That's a bed and breakfast inn. Don't y'all think that's a *marvelous* idea? Why, I have those seven extra bedrooms going to waste, and every day this town is full of people looking for a place to stay. As it is, the only place for miles is that tacky old Green Door Motel out by the bypass. Why, it's just not fitting for the caliber of folks who are frequenting our lovely town. Sure, they can go over to Mount Pine to the Marriott, but who wants to drive way over there? I could put a good many of those fine people up for the night, and in the morning I could serve them my famous French toast casserole and a fruit compote, then send them out to sightsee and shop in our fine Lovington establishments. Mama and Daddy would be so proud! Daddy always said, 'Eulalee, when are you going to make something of yourself?' I say, well, Daddy, better late than never!"

Then Miss Eulalee turned and hurried out the door, headed on back home to figure out how to turn her mama and daddy's house into a bed and breakfast place, so all the folks visiting Lovington—well, at least seven rooms of them at a time—would have a place to stay and eat French toast casserole. And a fruit compote.

FOUR

A Job that Doesn't Require Driving

Mama had left early for The Quilt Stop to get ready for the next busload of tourists, and Daddy had an emergency electrical call over in Mount Pine. Buddy was fishing with Wisteria's brother Luke down at the river, and I was home alone, eating Froot Loops and watching our new TV. Mama and Miss Nelda's quilt-selling business was doing so good, Mama had not only been able to buy our family a new television, she had also gotten herself the best top-of-the-line Kenmore washer and dryer set over at the Sears store in Mount Pine.

She said, "Thank goodness, 'cause I'm tired of kicking that old washer every time I want to get it started."

I heard Wisteria coming, whooping and hollering, before she hit the front yard. She came running up on the porch and bang, bang, banged on the door.

"Let me in. I got the best news!"

I was still in my pajamas, hadn't combed my hair or brushed my teeth. Hadn't even washed the sleep out of my eyes.

"What in the world, Wisteria?" I said, when I opened the door and found her sporting clean overalls and tee shirt, with her hair

27

in neat, new braids. She was hopping up and down, all red-faced from running, her braids jumping up and down on her back.

"Look! Just look at what I found when me and Mama were in the Piggly Wiggly this morning!"

She was waving a poster in my face so fast and close that I couldn't tell what it was all about.

I grabbed her wrist and said, "Hold still so I can see what it is."

"A festival! It's the Fall Is Just Around the Corner Festival! Look at it! Isn't it exciting? I am so hepped up I can hardly stand still."

She wasn't standing still at all.

"I've never been to a Fall Is Just Around the Corner Festival, and I just know there's so much fun to be had. Looky, Bit, there's rides to ride on and games of chance to play. They have exhibits and a whole midway full of food to eat. Doesn't that sound like the most fun imaginable?"

Wisteria is an excitable sort, but I'd never seen her this excited before.

"Wisteria, the Fall Is Just Around the Corner Festival comes to Lovington every year. I've been going for as long as I can remember."

"You mean to tell me you have attended this wonderful event numerous times," she yelled, waving the poster in my face, "and you never even bothered to mention it to me, your best friend? I'm pretty sure our best-friend contract states that you must share news of any such events with me."

"Well, it never dawned on me to tell you, and I don't recall mention of it in our best-friend contract. But, hey, we'll go to the Fall Is Just Around the Corner Festival, and we'll have a real good time, I promise. It's a lot of fun."

But not as much fun as Wisteria was making it out to be. I was hoping she wouldn't be disappointed.

"Well, I have a plan," she said.

"What kind of plan?"

"We need to get jobs."

"Jobs?"

"Yes, jobs, so we can make enough money by the time the Fall is Just Around the Corner Festival gets here to ride all the rides we want to ride, eat all the food we want to eat, see all the exhibits we want to see, and play all the games of chance we want to play."

"But, Wisteria, we're not old enough to get jobs. And we don't know how to do anything."

"Well, we're not gonna apply to be brain surgeons or accountants or beauticians, but there's plenty of things we know how to do. Surely, somebody would hire us because of our many talents. And with all those yella-headed ladies flocking to the stores down on Main Street, I know all the businesses are short-handed. I bet each and every one of 'em would be glad to have two very talented, dependable young ladies working for them."

"Wisteria, I don't know many people who need the services of a tap-dancing pollywog, do you?"

"But my swimming and tap-dancing are only two of my many talents. I can do lots of other stuff, I'm sure."

While I stood there listening to Wisteria's plan to get a job so we could earn money to go to the Fall Is Just Around the Corner Festival, my Froot Loops had gotten all puffy and soggy. I don't like puffy and soggy cereal of any kind, so I took my bowl into the kitchen and dumped the contents down the disposal, ground it up, rinsed my bowl and spoon, and put them in the dishwasher.

Wisteria followed me so close she stepped on my bare heel with her orange high-top, stopped just long enough to say, "'Scuse me," and kept on yakking about us getting jobs.

Knowing she wasn't going to let up until I agreed with her, I said, "Okay, Wisteria, so where do we start?"

"Well, as you know, I never come unprepared. I have a plan. First, we make a bunch of flyers—I'm guessing about twenty will do—that say we're looking for jobs. Then we hand them out to all the businesses in town."

"Sounds like a good start to me. So go get a marker and some paper out of Daddy's desk drawer and start designing our flyer while I go wash my face and brush my teeth and put on some clothes."

When I got back from getting dressed, I saw Wisteria laying flat on her stomach on the living room floor, humming some tuneless tune, concentrating real hard with her tongue sticking out the side of her mouth. Her feet were in the air, and she clacked her orange high-tops together while seriously designing our flyer.

"Well, what do you think?" she asked, handing her work to me when I came back in the living room.

"Not bad, Wisteria. Maybe you can get a job making flyers."

"Har har, very funny."

Her flyer read:

LOOKING FOR WORK
MONDAY THROUGH FRIDAY
BIT SIZEMORE AND
WISTERIA CALLIOPE JONES

STRONG, SMART, POLITE, LOYAL

AVAILABLE DURING SUMMER ONLY
SINCE WE HAVE TO GO TO SCHOOL
CALL 555-212-3113

"Looks real good, don't you think?"

"Yeah, but what if folks need us on Saturday or Sunday?"

"Well, too bad. Mama and Daddy Earl would never agree to me working on the Sabbath. That day is saved for Sunday school and church. And, Bit, we gotta have our Saturdays for being best friends."

"Yeah, you're right about that," I said, studying her flyer real hard. Then I said, "Uh oh, you missed one thing."

"What's that?"

"What if somebody needs us to drive them somewhere, like over to the bypass or to Mount Pine to go shopping at Belks Department Store or something?"

"Hmm, good point. Didn't think of that," she said, flopping back down on her belly and grabbing her marker. "We'll fix that."

LOOKING FOR WORK
MONDAY THROUGH FRIDAY
BIT SIZEMORE AND
WISTERIA CALLIOPE JONES

STRONG, SMART, POLITE, LOYAL

AVAILABLE DURING SUMMER ONLY
SINCE WE HAVE TO GO TO SCHOOL
CALL 555-212-3113

NO JOBS REQUIRING DRIVING CARS,
PLEASE!

"Perfect," I told her.

"Great! I knew you'd like it." And pulling out another sheet of paper, she said, "Only nineteen more to go."

"Wisteria, you don't have to make all the flyers by hand. Uncle Ted's got a copy machine, remember? I'm sure he won't mind us using it."

"Oh, silly me," Wisteria said, and bonked herself on the forehead with the heel of her hand.

Uncle Ted keeps a copy machine in the back of his drugstore, just in case anybody in Lovington needs to make a copy of something. He charges only a nickel a copy and says that doesn't even cover the cost of paper and electricity to run the machine or to make repairs. And that nickel charge is on the honor system. Uncle Ted has a little cardboard box back by the copy machine. When people make copies, they just drop their money in the little box. Leastwise, that's what they're supposed to do.

But he said, "It's the least I can do for all the folks who have given me a hand over the years."

So Wisteria and I struck off down the holler road to town, hoping Uncle Ted would think that Wisteria and I had given him a hand from time to time.

"Hey, Uncle Ted," I yelled across the drugstore when we came through the door. "Wisteria and I have a business proposition."

"Come on back and present your proposition to me while I'm filling prescriptions."

So we stepped up into Uncle Ted's prescription-filling office, and I said, "Well, me and Wisteria need a job. We want to go to the Fall Is Just Around the Corner Festival, and we figure it's gonna take a lot of money to ride all the rides we want to ride and eat all the food we want to eat and see all the exhibits we want to see and play all the games of chance we want to play."

"Y'all are probably right about that, so how do I fit in here?"

"We need to use your copy machine to make our flyers, advertising our services. Now, we can't pay you up front for the use of your machine. What we can do is pay you back, with interest, once we get a job and get our first paychecks. Is that a good business proposition?"

"Yes, that sounds like a very good business proposition, but let me make a counter proposal."

"Okay, we're all ears," Wisteria said.

So Uncle Ted told us, "Lots of people helped me get my business off the ground, and I've always wanted to do the same, help out someone else who is just getting her business started. So why don't we call the use of my copy machine my contribution to the start-up of your cottage industry?"

I didn't quite follow all that business-talk, but it sure sounded to me like Uncle Ted was giving us the use of his copy machine for free. I couldn't think of a better proposition till he added, "And I'll even throw in the paper."

"Yikes!" Wisteria screamed.

Wisteria is the only person I've ever known to say the word *yikes*. I thought it was just a word used in comic books, in a bubble over peoples' heads, to show somebody's excitement.

Uncle Ted said, "You girls know how to use the machine. Go on back, and call me if you run into a problem. And look underneath. There are lots of colors of paper to choose from."

We went on back to the rear of Uncle Ted's drugstore, and Wisteria went to rummaging for paper underneath the copy machine.

"Yellow," she said. "Only reasonable choice. Reminds me of sunshine. It will make people happy when they see it and will make them want to give us a job. Don't you agree?"

I did agree and figured that the red and green looked like Christmas and the purple was too dark. And I knew why Wisteria didn't want the pink, but she resisted saying *damn sissy.* Guess she thought it wouldn't be businesslike. So yellow it was, and we cranked out about twenty copies, deciding that would be enough to spread around town.

We took our flyers to Uncle Ted to get his approval, since he was an investor—well, the *only* investor—in our cottage industry.

"Perfect," he said. "I predict you'll be employed before the day is over."

"Thanks, Uncle Ted," we said, and headed out to apply for a job.

We went into every store, and even the post office and Doc Spivey's office, and said, "Hi, we are Bit Sizemore and Wisteria Calliope Jones," even though everybody in Lovington already knew who we were, "and we are looking for work. We'll just leave our flyer with you so you can think about maybe giving us a job."

When we went into the post office, O.O.—that's Miss Opal Offenbacker, the post mistress—was sorting mail into mail slots.

O.O. is a mighty fine lady. Everybody in Lovington thinks so. She's lived all by herself down in the woods ever since her daddy got killed in an awful truck accident, so many years back. But she's real kind, even buys shoes every Christmas for all the poor kids up in the holler. Why, O.O. even foiled a robbery over at Mr. Fisher's filling station one time. She yanked the gun out of the robber's hand, bonked him upside the head with it, and had him crying before the whole thing was over. So she's sort of a folk hero here in Lovington.

"What brings you girls in this morning?" she asked us.

So Wisteria said, "Well, Miss O.O., we're in need of a job and thought you might could use a hand around here."

Miss O.O. smiled and said, "As much as I could use a good hand around here, and I don't doubt for a minute that you girls could handle the job, we got ourselves a big problem."

"What's that, Miss O.O.?" Wisteria said.

"Y'all know this is a government facility, right?"

"Right," we both said.

"Well, in order to work in a government facility, you gotta first take the Civil Service exam."

"No problem-o," Wisteria said. "me and Bit are both real good at test taking. We could ace that thing," she said, having no idea what kind of questions were on a Civil Service exam.

"Wish it were that easy, Wisteria, but I'm afraid you and Bit here just don't qualify age-wise. You gotta be twenty-one to take the test. Either of you twenty-one?"

"'Fraid not," Wisteria said, the corners of her mouth all turned down.

"Didn't reckon you were, but I thought I'd best check, just to make sure," Miss O.O. said.

"That's okay, Miss O.O. Rules are rules," Wisteria said to her.

"But I tell you what," Miss O.O. said, "I want to help out you young businesswomen any way I can. So take this here roll of Scotch tape, and stick your flyer in the front window, right where anybody passing by or coming in will see it."

So we did like Miss O.O. said and stuck one of our yellow flyers in the front window of the post office.

"Thank you, Miss O.O. We appreciate it."

"My pleasure, girls. I wish you luck in your search for employment. And don't you two be strangers. It gets a might lonely down here in the post office."

We assured Miss O.O. that we wouldn't be strangers and were on our way to visit with the rest of the merchants on Main Street in Lovington.

Most folks said they weren't in the market to hire right that minute since they'd already done their hiring when the economy of Lovington had started to boom. But they did all say that they'd give it some serious thought since they were certain we'd be good, hard workers. Everybody took a flyer, though, most of them saying they'd be glad to display them in their front windows, just like Miss O.O.

When we got to Mama and Miss Nelda's quilt store, the two of them looked frazzled, trying to stock shelves and take care of all the customers by themselves.

Wisteria said, "Hi, Miss Brenda, hi, Miss Nelda, we are Bit Sizemore and Wisteria Calliope Jones, and we are looking for work. This here is our flyer."

Miss Nelda said, "Pleased to meet you, Wisteria and Bit." Then she took a copy of our flyer and looked it over. "Very good," she said.

Mama didn't even bother to look at our flyer before she raked her sleeve across her perspiring forehead and said, "You're hired."

"Huh?"

"We'll work out the details later—hours, wages, and whatnot—but for now, start stocking these shelves. Y'all have hung around here underfoot long enough to know how it's done and where everything goes. Now, get to work."

And just like that, we had a job. We worked our be-hinds off that very first day, doing anything Mama and Miss Nelda needed done. At the end of the afternoon, Wisteria and I dragged ourselves out to Mama's car. Wisteria fell face-down onto the back seat, and I had to fold her legs up to get the door shut. Then I crawled into the front seat and closed my eyes. Mama drove Wisteria to the rickety little trailer down by the river, and she had to wake her up when we got there.

"Wisteria, honey, you think you can make it inside all by yourself?"

"Yes, ma'am," she said, just above a whisper, and oozed out of the car real slow and sorta weaved her way up to the front door.

When I got home, I told Mama I was going to bed.

"No, Bit. If you don't eat some supper, you won't have enough energy down at the shop tomorrow. And Nelda and I are going to need for you and Wisteria to be energetic and alert if you're going to work for us. Now, run take your bath. Supper will be ready by the time you're finished. Now, scoot."

By the time I was out of the bath, Daddy and Buddy were home. Instead of putting my clothes back on, I pulled on my pajamas and came to the supper table looking like I was ready for bed. My daddy and brother gabbed with Mama about their day, but I just sort of half-listened and ate my supper. I think it was pot roast, but I was really too sleepy to tell for sure.

After supper I went to my room and fell into bed. At least, I think that's what I did since that's where I was the next morning when Mama stuck her head in my door and said, "Up and at 'em, Bit. We gotta get to work."

And that's how me and Wisteria's working careers got started. Soon, though, we got the hang of it all and could do our jobs in our sleep. We knew better than anybody every little thing that was in The Quilt Shop, even better than Mama and Miss Nelda, and we knew where it all belonged, how much it cost, and how best to display it for all the customers who filled The Quilt Shop every day. We stocked shelves, arranged the window displays, ran errands, waited on customers, rang up the cash register, tagged items, dusted shelves, and dusted inventory. You name it, we did it. I won't say we weren't pooped by the end of each day, but we were hard-working girls with real jobs—just like our flyer promised we'd be—and we were earning money so we could go to the Fall Is Just Around the Corner Festival.

FIVE

Sweet Baby Jesus
on a June Bug

Mama had asked Wisteria and me to run some errands for her once we'd finished our lunch over at Uncle Ted's. We'd just left the drugstore and were heading down to Mr. Hammitt's hardware store when we came upon two men we hadn't ever seen before. They were out washing the windows on the old Peabody Furniture Store, which hadn't been in business since before I was born. Over the door, where the old, faded Peabody Furniture Store sign used to be, hung a new sign that read *Antiques and Junque.*

"Hi, what'cha doin'?" Wisteria asked the men.

One of the men stopped, pulled a rag out of his hip pocket, wiped off his squeegee, and said, "We're preparing to open an antique store here in the old Peabody Building."

I said, "Hi, I'm Bit Sizemore, and this is my best friend, Wisteria Calliope Jones."

"Sizemore, Sizemore," the man said, squinching up his forehead and tapping his chin with his finger. "How do I know that name?"

Then the other man turned around and said, "Brenda Sizemore? The Quilt Shop lady?"

"Oh, of course, you must be Brenda's daughter."

"Yes, sir, I am."

"Pardon my manners," said the man holding the squeegee, "I'm Wilson Murchison, and this is Ralston Tanninger. I grew up near here, over in Mount Pine. I left shortly after I graduated from high school since there wasn't much of interest for me in Mount Pine."

He sorta chuckled and waved his hand around in the air when he said that, like it was some kind of inside joke that I should know.

"I met Ralston when I went to New York to work in the theatre. We owned an antique store in the city for a good many years. But we heard how Lovington was booming with business possibilities, so we decided to relocate our antique shop down here and take our chances. Ralston and I are risk takers, always ready for an adventure."

Wisteria let out a laugh and said, "Well, I don't think of Lovington and adventure as synonymous, but to each his own..."

Then Mr. Ralston came over and stuck out his hand. "I'm real excited to be here. And it's good to meet our first new friends. Hi, Bit. Hi, Wisteria. Would you care to come in and have a Coke with us? We were just discussing taking a break."

"Sure, that would be great," Wisteria said and charged past Mr. Wilson and Mr. Ralston, right into their store.

"Sweet baby Jesus on a June bug!" Wisteria screamed. "Where did all this crap come from? And how did you get it all into town without me seeing it? Doesn't much get past me."

Both Mr. Wilson and Mr. Ralston laughed at Wisteria's brashness, and Mr. Ralston said, "We sneaked it in under the cover of darkness."

"I believe it," Wisteria said, "but it must've took a whole bunch of big trucks and a lot of darkness to get it here undetected."

While Wisteria was running wild all over the store, touching all the knick-knacks and do-dads, Mr. Wilson reached into a big old red antique Co-Cola chest full of ice and pulled out four little bottles of Co-Cola. He wiped them off with a red-checkered dish towel and popped off the tops with the bottle opener that was attached to the edge of the drink chest.

"Here you go, girls," he said, and Wisteria appeared by his side to claim her bottle of Co-Cola. She was wearing a purple felt hat that came all the way down to the tops of her eyes. It had a great big green feather sticking out the side.

"Thanks, Mr. Wilson," she said. "I've never seen anything like this. It's gonna take me about forever to examine every little thing you got in this store. And I aim to do just that."

"Well, you take your time, Wisteria. We'd love to have you examine every little thing."

"By the way," my nosy friend said, "where'd y'all find to live? Lovington is overrun with people and no place to put 'em."

"There's an apartment right upstairs, over the store," Mr. Ralston told her. "We're making our home up there."

"Neat," said Wisteria, and went on back to plundering through Mr. Wilson and Mr. Ralston's stuff.

Finally, I said, "Thanks for the Co-Colas, but me and Wisteria have some errands to run for my mama." And I called out, "Wisteria, go put that hat back where you found it, and come on."

While Wisteria was returning the purple hat, I said, "I hope you'll stop by The Quilt Shop sometime. I know Mama and Miss Nelda would like to meet y'all."

"We'll do that," they both said, and walked us outside and started back to cleaning their store windows.

* * *

That night we had a potluck supper on the grounds at our church. Wisteria came along with me because I promised her there wouldn't be any wine drinking going on.

When we got there, Wisteria headed straight for the dessert table, grabbed a Dixie paper plate, and helped herself to a piece of Miss Nelda's pineapple upside down cake.

So I said, "Wisteria, you haven't even eaten your supper yet. You're gonna spoil your appetite."

"Like I always say, Bit, eat dessert first so you won't run the risk of filling up that dessert hole with green bean casserole."

Miss Nelda came up and said, "Wisteria, you want me to hold your cake till you finish your supper?"

"No, ma'am, I'd rather eat just the cake."

"Well, honey, I think you need more than that. You want to put some meat on those bones, don't you?"

And I leaned over and whispered, "You might even put some boobs on that flat chest of yours."

So she said, "Oh, okay, Miss Nelda, but don't go far with that pineapple upside down cake 'cause I'll be back for it soon."

"Okay, Wisteria," Miss Nelda said, chuckling and shaking her head.

"All right, I'll eat some friend chicken, but I refuse to eat any old cheesy broccoli or that disgusting green bean casserole. I'm not running the risk of filling up my dessert hole."

When we got to the supper table, Miss Pearline Troutman was putting out her antique silver plate full of Vi-enna sausages wrapped up in Pillsbury refrigerator dough. I don't care if she does put them on her antique silver plate, they're still just yucky old Vi-enna sausages wrapped in dough.

"Hey, Miss Pearline, how you tonight?" Wisteria asked.

"I'm quite fine, Wisteria, Bit. I understand you two young ladies have been keeping company with some of Lovington's new residents," she said with that I-don't-approve-at-all-of-your-behavior air about her. She had her bright red fingernails resting on her great big bosoms and leaning together like *here's the church, here's the steeple,* and her nostrils were all flared out so you could look all up inside her nose.

"Which residents are you talking about, Miss Pearline? We know all the residents of Lovington," I said.

"Those gentlemen who have opened that antique store in the old Peabody building, right down from your dear Uncle Ted's drugstore."

"Oh, you mean Mr. Wilson and Mr. Ralston," I said.

"Those are the ones. Do your parents know you've been associating with them?"

"Well, I don't know about us associating, seeing as how we just saw them the one time," Wisteria said.

"Quite frankly, I don't think it is at all appropriate for young ladies to be seen with *those* kinds of people."

"What do you mean by *those kinds of people?*" I asked, real confused.

"Unnatural people. They're engaged in an unnatural relationship."

"I don't understand what you mean, Miss Pearline."

"Well, then, go ask your mother," she sniffed at me. Then she popped one of her nasty Vi-enna sausages in her mouth and walked away real fast.

So Wisteria and I both grabbed a fried chicken leg and went running to locate my mama. I found her talking to Father Frank, so I tugged on her sleeve and gave her our squinty-eye look that meant I needed to talk to her.

She said, "Pardon me, Father Frank, it seems Bit and Wisteria need me for something."

Then she turned around and said kinda stern-like, "What's so important, Bit?"

"What is an *unnatural relationship?*"

"What are you talking about?"

"Miss Pearline said Wisteria and I shouldn't be associating with the likes of Mr. Wilson and Mr. Ralston down at the Antiques and Junque store 'cause they are engaged in an *unnatural relationship*. What does that mean?"

Mama got a real slit-eyed angry look—which is a far cry from a squinty-eye I-have-to-talk-to-you look—on her face. With her jaw all clenched tight, she said, "Well, Mr. Wilson and Mr. Ralston are living like a married couple. Some people seem to think that they are living in an unnatural relationship since they can't have children."

Then Wisteria piped up and said, "Well, my Uncle Garvin and Aunt Trudy can't have children neither, and heaven knows they been trying hard for years. Does that mean they are engaged in an unnatural relationship?"

Mama pinched up her lips and said, "No, darlin', there's not a thing unnatural about your Uncle Garvin and Aunt Trudy—or Mr. Wilson and Mr. Ralston, for that matter. They're both couples who love each other and want to spend their lives together. And don't you girls be listening to Miss Pearline. She's just an old busybody. And you be kind and polite to everybody, you hear?"

"Yes, ma'am," we both said to Mama.

Just then Miss Pearline came up to us, and she said, "Brenda, I'm assuming the girls have told you what we discussed. I know those kinds of things are hard for parents to talk about with their children, but at least I planted the seed. I'm sure you understand."

"Yes, Miss Pearline, I understand very well that you are a busybody, and I don't appreciate one bit your filling my children's heads with your prejudices. In the future, please keep your opinions to yourself. I'll parent my children as I see fit. And don't you ever tell them who they can talk to and who they can be friends with. They have been taught to be kind and polite to everyone."

When Mama said that, Miss Pearline stretched her eyes real wide in astonishment. Then she started batting her stubby little eyelashes real fast. Without saying another word to my mama, she huffed real hard, clicked her red, here's-the-church-here's-the-steeple fingernails together, and went charging off toward the Vi-enna sausage table.

When it got real quiet, Wisteria said, "All right, then, have we got that all straightened out?"

Mama laughed and hugged Wisteria to her and said, "Yes, darlin', we got that all straightened out."

"Okay, then. I'm ready for my pineapple upside down cake now," Wisteria said, tossing her half-eaten chicken leg in the trash and heading for Miss Nelda, who was guarding her dessert.

SIX

Senator Compton
Comes A How 'doin'

Once Mama and Miss Nelda's quilt shop got to going gang-busters, Enos Ransom came in with some of his wood carvings of ducks and deer and whatnot and said he wondered if anybody might be interested in buying them. Mama and Miss Nelda said it wouldn't hurt to try and that he was welcome to display his work at The Quilt Shop. Pretty soon Enos's carvings were flying off the shelves. The tourists called it primitive art.

Mr. Murdock decided if Enos could sell his stuff, he could probably sell his wooden bird houses. Sure enough, those city folks just couldn't live without a Henry Murdock bird house. Didn't matter what folks brought in to sell—needlepoint pillows, crocheted tea cozies, smocked baby dresses—that's what the yella-headed ladies wanted.

So Wisteria and I were in the stock room one morning not long after Mama and Miss Nelda hired us, putting price stickers on bird houses and crocheted placemats and baby bonnets made out of handkerchiefs and lord knows what else. Mama wanted us to get them on the shelves before the next busload of ladies pulled into town.

We heard a whole bunch of ruckus and a real loud man's voice coming from the front of the store, so we stuck our heads out the stock-room to see what was going on.

The man with the real deep voice was walking around the shop, shaking hands and smiling real big, saying, "How 'do," and "Glad to make your acquaintance," and "Good to see you," and "Everything goin' all right over here in Lovington?"

Now, we didn't get many men coming in The Quilt Shop, just ladies in sensible shoes. So this loud-talking, teeth-showing, hand-shaking man was a mystery to me and Wisteria.

"Who you suppose that is?" Wisteria asked, still peeping around the stock-room door.

"Don't really know, but there's something about him that looks mighty familiar."

Just then Mama caught sight of me and Wisteria spying on her customer, and she motioned for us to come on out.

"Bit, Wisteria, come out here a minute. There's some people here I'd like for y'all to meet."

Wisteria and I shrugged at each other, put down the baby bonnets, and went to the front of the store.

"Senator and Mrs. Compton, I'd like for you to meet my daughter, Bit, and her best friend, Wisteria Jones. They're working here in the store over their summer break."

Mrs. Compton was real pretty with her white hair pulled back in a ponytail and her face all made up, her lips real pink and shiny.

She smiled gentle-like and said, real sweet and whispery, "Hi, Bit, Wisteria, I'm so glad to meet you."

Then Senator Compton near about yelled, "Well, how 'do, little ladies. My pleasure. I bet you're making your mamas and daddies mighty proud, holding down a job over your summer vacation. It'll do you good, give you character."

"It'll give us enough money so we can go to the Fall Is Just Around the Corner Festival," Wisteria told Senator Compton.

He threw back his head real far and let out a loud laugh. "Why, you're a real caution, young lady."

Then he took my hand and patted it like I was a puppy. "Good to meet you, too, sugar."

Wisteria rolled her eyes at me and said, "We got work to do."

I poked her in the back and said, "Nice to meet you, Mrs. Compton, Senator Compton. I hope you enjoy your stay." Then I smiled real sweet and said, "I guess me and Wisteria better get on back to work."

When we got out of earshot, Wisteria hissed, "How 'do? Sugar? Who does that old blow-hard think we are, some old hillbilly hicks?"

"And why the heck is he patting my hand like I'm a puppy and acting so big and important? I'm not even a voter," I added.

Then Wisteria said, "And you better believe if I was able to vote, that smiley old I'm-just-a-good-old-boy Compton sure wouldn't be getting my vote!"

Just then Mama stuck her head around the corner and said, "Pipe down, girls, and be polite."

"But, Mama, he acts like we're just a bunch of stupid, country hicks, with all his how 'doin'."

"Well, play nice and smile real sweet. That's our bread and butter. Mrs. Compton is showing serious interest in three of my quilts."

"I'd rather not sell quilts," I said, putting on my pouty face.

"You have a job, Bit, because I sell quilts. And remember this conversation the next time you watch that new TV. Now, get back to work. We have quilts to sell, to anybody who wants to buy them," Mama said and raised her eyebrow at me in an I-don't-want-any-more-of-your-sass kind of way.

"Ladies," Senator Compton was saying to my mama and Miss Nelda, "I don't get up to these parts often enough. I didn't know what I was missing. This is the most beautiful area of our fair state."

I was guessing he said that no matter where he was in our fair state at any given minute. He had to please and flatter those local voters.

Then he said to Mrs. Compton, loud enough for all the shop to hear," I believe I'll take me a ride around and get a good look at beautiful Lovington. Would that be okay with you, Mother?"

"Why, yes, Fletch, you go right ahead. I'll stay here and shop. And then at lunch time I'll stroll down to that little sidewalk café we saw when we drove into town."

"Very well, Mother, I'll return for you soon."

Once Senator Compton made sure he had said, "How 'do?" to everybody, he left Mrs. Compton to go check out fair and beautiful Lovington.

He climbed into his big old black Lexus and took off up the holler. He kept on till he got to Mose Beemus's place, about two miles up the holler road from where I live.

Mose said Senator Compton wheeled on into his driveway, just like he'd been invited for a visit. Fact is, Mose hadn't ever laid eyes on Fletcher Compton—except on television—and certainly hadn't asked him in for a glass of sweet tea.

Senator Compton oozed out of his car, and, without even introducing himself, said to Mose, who was digging in his vegetable garden, "Howdy, my friend! You own this land?"

Word has it that when the senator said that, without looking up from his digging, Mose said, "Who wants to know? And I ain't your friend."

Senator Compton just assumed that everybody knew who he was; truth be told, Mose knew exactly who Fletcher Compton was. But he didn't take to anybody coming to visit unannounced and uninvited and calling him a friend when he didn't even know him from Adam, especially when the somebody was a senator Mose hadn't voted for.

Senator Compton put his politician's face back on, flashing his perfect teeth, shaking Mose's hand, introducing himself, and telling Mose how beautiful his property was. Pretty soon he and Mose were tight, good buddies and all.

Daddy says some folks are suckers for flattery...and a big fat wallet.

Mose told Senator Compton that his house was the last one up the holler and that he owned all the land beyond his house for as far as you could drive and then some—and, boy howdy, that's a lot of land.

Senator Compton said, "How'd you feel about selling me a sizeable plot of your land?"

Without hesitating one split second, Mose said, "I ain't got no heirs, and I ain't gittin' no younger. I can't take it with me, and it ain't doin' me no good. Maybe we can cut us a deal."

Daddy said it sounded awful suspicious, like Mose had been looking for a buyer all along.

Fletcher Compton told Mose that he had been searching for some land to build himself a hunting lodge and that Mose's property seemed to be just what he had in mind. Before the day was out, the two men had struck a deal, Senator Compton had himself some land, and Mose was a whole lot richer.

Mose said, "I'd sell him all the land he wanted, but I still wouldn't vote for that old windbag."

Soon as Mose had signed on the dotted line, the construction trucks and construction workers started heading up the holler. Fletcher Compton planned to have himself a hunting lodge that would sleep sixteen people by fall hunting season, and before then Mose Beemus would be living in town in a brand new, two-bedroom townhouse with indoor plumbing, electrical heat, and a one-car garage—and not one bit of acreage to mow or plow or tend to in any way.

* * *

Not long after Senator Compton and Mose Beemus struck their deal, Wisteria and I were walking to work early one morning. Going down the holler road, we counted seven construction trucks of some sort or another, heading in the opposite direction, all of 'em kicking up dust as they rumbled by. The trucks were going up the holler to build Senator Compton's hunting lodge.

By the time we got to The Quilt Shop, we were covered in dust and our throats were coated and dry. We brushed ourselves off best we could and headed inside for a drink of water.

"Hey, Mama, hey, Miss Nelda, those trucks are kicking up an awful lot of dust up the holler road. I'll be glad when that dang hunting lodge is finally built," I called out as Wisteria and I headed for the water fountain back by the bathroom.

Halfway to the back of the store, I heard someone say, "Sorry that hunting lodge is giving you problems."

I stopped dead in my tracks when I saw the prettiest boy I'd ever laid my eyes on. He was sort of tall, and he had light blonde hair that hung over to one side. His eyes were the biggest and brightest blue I'd ever seen. His smile was real wide, so wide it showed off his straight, white teeth.

I just stood and stared at him without saying a word, so he shook his hair back and said, "Hi, I'm Palmer Lee Compton. My dad is the one building the hunting lodge. Sorry it's bothering you."

"Oh, n-no, it's not bothering me," I stammered. "Me and my friend, Wisteria, just got all dusty from the construction trucks driving up the holler road, that's all."

Wisteria poked me in the back and said, "Come on, let's go get a drink of water to wash all that dust out of our throats."

I ignored her and said, "Hey, Palmer Lee. I'm Bit Sizemore, and this is my best friend, Wisteria Calliope Jones. We work here. That's my mama up there."

Palmer Lee stuck out his hand and said, "Nice to meet you, Bit. You too, Wisteria."

I shook his hand. I had never shook hands with another kid before. It seemed so grown up. Palmer Lee seemed so grown up. And so handsome.

Wisteria didn't shake his hand but just stood there impatient-like with her hands on her skinny little hips and her eyes all slitty.

When I didn't say anything, Palmer Lee said, "I'm here with my parents," and he motioned to his mama who was going through a stack of quilts at the front of the store.

I called, "Hey, Mrs. Compton," and she looked up and smiled and waved and said, "Hello, Bit."

"So you've already met my mother?"

"Oh, sure. Your mama has come in shopping before. She's real sweet and pretty."

"Thanks, Bit, I'll tell her you said so." Then he leaned close and kinda whispered out the corner of his mouth, "But you do realize that politician's wives *have* to be sweet and pretty, don't you?"

I giggled and then asked him, "Are you staying over at Miss Eulalee's?"

"You mean the B&B down the street?"

"Yeah, that's Miss Eulalee's old homeplace. She just turned it into a B&B," I said, rambling, not really knowing how to talk to a boy who shakes hands like a grown-up.

"Yes, that's where we're staying."

"Did she serve you her famous French toast casserole and fruit compote this morning?"

"As a matter of fact, she did. She says that tomorrow we'll be having egg casserole and cheese grits. Mmm, can't wait."

I laughed for the second time at Palmer Lee, and my dry throat turned even dryer. I said, "Excuse me, I need a drink of water. And then we need to get to work. Nice meeting you, Palmer Lee."

"Hey, wait, just one more thing...I can't seem to get my phone to work around here. Do you know what the problem is?"

"Palmer Lee, we don't have a tower here in Lovington, so we just don't get cell phone service."

"You're kidding."

"Nope, 'fraid not. And we don't have cable either. The only way to get more than the one TV channel from over in Mount Pine is to put a DISH on top of the house."

Palmer Lee just stood there, like he'd been slapped into another dimension.

"Wow," was all he said.

"Yeah, some might say Lovington is sorta off the grid."

I heard Wisteria clear her throat, so I said, "Well, I really do need to get to work. Nice meeting you, Palmer Lee."

"Oh, sure. Nice meeting you too. Maybe I'll see you again soon."

"Yeah," was all I had left in me.

Wisteria and I headed for the water fountain. I looked back once and saw that Palmer Lee hadn't moved and was still staring at me. It made me sort of uncomfortable, but it also made my stomach do butterflies.

And all of a sudden, I was real sorry I hadn't dressed a little nicer for work, maybe done something special to my hair. Palmer Lee was all dressed up in khaki Bermudas and a button-down shirt. Me, I was wearing old blue jeans and my blue and gold pep club tee shirt that said Lovington High School Cougars on it. And I'd just washed my curly hair and let it dry natural, and it was kinda bouffing out all over my head. But there wasn't a thing I could do about it now.

But he'd said, "Maybe I'll see you again soon."

Well, when *again soon* came, I'd make sure I wasn't wearing jeans and a tee shirt.

After we'd rinsed the dust out of our throats, Wisteria and I set about stocking shelves. We'd move from shelf to shelf, and Palmer Lee's eyes would follow me. I'd look over, and he'd smile real big.

By the time his mama said, "Come on, Palmer Lee, I need to get over to the drugstore," I was bright red with embarrassment, and the perspiration was breaking out on my lip and my armpits.

SEVEN

Purdy Boy Moves in on Wisteria's Time

"Bit, the phone's for you," Buddy yelled from the kitchen. I was practicing my piano lesson, and I was glad for a break. I actually thought I deserved a whole summer break, but my piano teacher thought different.

"But, Miss Mercy, we have vacation from school. And Wisteria has vacation from tap dancing lessons. Why don't I get vacation from piano lessons?"

"It doesn't work that way, Bit. You know very well that if you don't play regularly, you'll lose your touch. And with your talent, you know you don't want to lose your touch."

It was true. I did play the piano real good, good enough for school assemblies and the little kids' Sunday school. I even competed in the state piano competition over at the Capital, and I sure didn't want to lose my touch. But sometimes I got tired of practicing, especially when the piece I was working on was real challenging. And Miss Mercy loved challenging me. She always believed I was up to the task.

But when the phone rang and Buddy yelled that it was for me, I banged down the piano lid and ran to the kitchen, figuring Wisteria was calling about something.

"Hey, what's up?"

"Bit?" the caller said, but it wasn't Wisteria.

"'Scuse me," I said, real embarrassed, "I thought you were my friend, Wisteria. Who's this?"

"Well, it isn't Wisteria. It's Palmer Lee Compton."

Palmer Lee Compton? That cute senator's son I'd met down at The Quilt Shop that morning? I just couldn't talk. Cat got my tongue, as they say. I didn't get calls from boys, unless it was about homework or the homecoming committee. And I *never* got calls from cute senators' sons.

"Bit, are you there?"

"Um, yeah, I'm right here. You just surprised me is all. Like I said, I was expecting a call from Wisteria."

I really wasn't, but it was the only thing I could think to say.

"Nope, not Wisteria," he said.

"Well, then, hey there, Palmer Lee. I see you found a phone."

"Yeah, I'm using the one in Miss Eulalee's parlor 'cause it's the only one in the house."

"I'm sure Miss Eulalee doesn't mind you using it."

"She said it was okay. But she said it was for all her guests, so not to hang on the line too long."

I just laughed at Miss Eulalee lecturing Senator Compton's son.

"So the reason I'm calling is because I was wondering if you'd like to go to a movie. I noticed there's a theatre right near your mama's store."

"Palmer Lee, my mama and daddy don't allow me to date. I'm not old enough. I'm only fourteen, won't be fifteen for two more months."

"Oh, I'm sorry. I thought you were at least sixteen."

I felt myself blush at the thought that an older boy believed I was older than I really was. I was so glad he couldn't see my face turning red.

"Nope, just fourteen. How old are you?"

"Sixteen, as of Tuesday."

"Well, happy birthday, Palmer Lee. Did you have a big party?"

"My mom and dad and I celebrated at Mr. Carl's diner with the pot roast special and apple pie."

I laughed and said, "That's not much of a party."

"Well, I gotta say, that apple pie was better than any birthday cake I've ever tasted."

"Yeah, Mr. Carl's mama makes all the pies for his restaurant. Wait till you taste her lemon meringue. That's her Sunday pie. But you gotta get there early 'cause it goes fast."

"That sounds good. Maybe you and I can go to Mr. Carl's for pie sometime. Not a date. Just friends. We can be friends, can't we?

"I guess so. Maybe you can come down to The Quilt Shop tomorrow, and you and Wisteria and I can go over to my Uncle Ted's drugstore and get a Cherry Co-Cola. You like Cherry Co-Colas?"

"Sure, that sounds great," Palmer Lee said. "Well, I'd better run. I'm going over to Asheville with my folks to some sort of fund raiser. So I guess I'll see you tomorrow."

"Yeah, see you tomorrow."

That night I couldn't think of a thing but Palmer Lee Compton. He was a big-city senator's son, and he liked me enough to call me on the phone and ask me to hang out. And he thought I was sixteen. I took a real long shower and shampooed my hair twice. I wanted to make sure I washed out all the construction dust. Then I went through my closet and picked out my favorite outfit to wear the next day. And it wasn't jeans and a Lovington Cougars tee shirt.

* * *

"What in tarnation are you doing dressed up like a damn sissy?" Wisteria asked when she stopped by for me the next morning on her way to work.

I had picked out my blue flowered skirt and a white tank and my gold sandals. I'd put my hair up in a ponytail, and I'd even put on a little pale pink lip gloss and some blush that I usually just wore to Sunday school.

"Just felt like it. I get tired of wearing jeans and a tee shirt all the time. We're girls. We ought to act like it from time to time."

"It's that boy, isn't it? That purdy boy, Palmer Lee. That's what it is," Wisteria said, all angry, with her fists on her hips, like she was accusing me of something.

"Well, yeah, maybe. He's coming back to The Quilt Shop today. We're going over to Uncle Ted's for a Cherry Co-Cola, and we want you to go with us."

"Well, damn, if I'd known that, maybe I'd have dressed up too."

"Sorry, Wisteria, I just didn't think to tell you. I'll remember next time."

"Never mind. You know damn well I'm not dressing up for any boy. I'll leave that to the sissies."

She stopped short of calling me, her best friend forever, a *damn* sissy.

"Okay, then, let's go." I said, "Mama said she and Miss Nelda are gonna be busy today, and they need our help real bad."

So Wisteria and I took off for work down the holler road, me in my skirt and sandals, Wisteria in her tee shirt and overalls with a hole in the knee.

About ten o'clock Palmer Lee showed up. I was so glad I'd dressed up. He had on shorts and a polo shirt. I was beginning to wonder if he even owned a pair of jeans.

When Wisteria saw him come in the door and say hi to Mama and Miss Nelda, she huffed and rolled her eyes and started stocking shelves real fast and hard.

"Hi," Palmer Lee said and smiled when he got to the back of the store.

"Hmmmm," was all Wisteria would say.

"Y'all want a Cherry Coke?"

"Sure. Come on, Wisteria. Let's go down to Uncle Ted's. Mama said we could take a break this morning."

"Nah, y'all go on. I got work to do."

"Oh, come on, Wisteria, go get a Cherry Co-Cola with us. We won't be long," I said.

"That's right, Wisteria," Palmer Lee kidded her, "we won't keep you away from your stocking for long."

"I said *no*! But thanks. Y'all go have your Cherry Co-Colas—and hurry back, Bit."

Then she turned around and went on back to flinging stuff onto shelves.

I shrugged at Palmer Lee and headed for the door.

"Mama, me and Palmer Lee are going down to Uncle Ted's for a Cherry Co-Cola. We won't be long."

"How about Wisteria, Bit? Don't you think she'd like to go too?"

I don't think Mama was too comfortable about me being with a boy all by myself. But I guess she figured since I was going to be under the watchful eye of my Uncle Ted, it'd be okay.

"We invited her, Mama, but she won't go."

Mama looked toward the back of the store where Wisteria was working away, and she said, "Well, okay, then. Hurry back."

"Thanks, Mama. I won't be too long."

"Doesn't Wisteria like me?" Palmer Lee asked, when we were out on the sidewalk.

"Well, I don't believe she even knows you. Maybe when y'all get better acquainted..."

I didn't know what else to say on the subject and was thinking she probably never would like Palmer Lee. I kinda got the notion that Wisteria's feelings were hurt because I was her best friend and she wanted me all to herself. But I didn't think that was fair. I figured I deserved to be friends with other people, just as long as she stayed my *best* friend.

"Uncle Ted, this is Palmer Lee Compton," I said when we went in the drugstore and found Uncle Ted behind the prescription counter.

"Hey, Palmer Lee," Uncle Ted said, coming around the counter and shaking his hand, not the least bit self-conscious about shaking hands with a kid. "You must be Senator Compton's son. Glad to meet you. Bit, Cherry Co-Colas are on me this morning. And make sure to take one to Wisteria when you go."

"Thanks, Uncle Ted."

"Hey, Selma," I said when we sat down at the counter, "this is Palmer Lee."

"Hi, Palmer Lee," she said, and to me she added, "and I understand the Cherry Co-Colas are on Uncle Ted this morning."

"Yes, ma'am, they are. As usual."

Selma just smiled and winked at me.

"What do y'all do for fun in Lovington?" Palmer Lee asked, as Selma placed our Cherry Co-Colas on the counter and I took a sip.

"Well, let's see, during school we go to football games and basketball games and baseball games. Sometimes we have dances in the cafetorium on Friday nights. And that pretty much takes up the whole school year. In the summer we usually go up to the pond and swim. The pond is up behind my house in a clearing in the woods. Our daddies tamped a path down for us to get to it, and then they built a dock for us to sit on and jump off into the water. Sometimes we'll take a picnic with us and eat it on the dock. Mostly, though, we play games in the water or paddle around on our floats. Course, if you don't like swimming, there's trout fishing up the holler in the river. But I don't like fishing."

"Sounds like fun."

"We also got the bowling alley over by the bypass, but Mama doesn't like us going out there too much. Some rough guys from over around Mount Pine come to bowl on weekends, and she doesn't think it's very safe for young girls to be there. And we've got the Fall Is Just Around the Corner Festival. That's real fun. But that's just once a year. And that's pretty much it for Lovington."

"Do you like to swim?" Palmer Lee asked.

"Sure, I'm a real good swimmer. Daddy taught me and Buddy to swim up at the pond before we could walk. At least that's what Daddy says."

"I like to swim too. I belong to the swim team at our school. But I haven't found a pool since we've been here."

"There's no pool in Lovington, Palmer Lee. But you can come up to the pond with me and Wisteria this Saturday, if you'd like? It's not a swimming pool, but it's real nice."

I realized when I said it that Saturday was Wisteria's and my time to be best friends, but I figured we'd have room for Palmer Lee up at the pond, at least this one Saturday.

"Sure, that sounds great."

Then I looked up at the Co-Cola clock behind the soda fountain and said, "Oops, I've been gone a long time. I gotta run. Wisteria needs my help."

"Okay, I'll walk you back," Palmer Lee said. He reached in his pocket and pulled out some change to leave on the counter for Selma.

"Thanks for the Cherry Coke, Selma," he said, as I picked up the drink she had fixed for me to take to Wisteria.

Selma smiled real big and raked her tip into her apron pocket and said, "Now, come back to see us, you hear, Palmer Lee?"

"Yes, ma'am, I will."

When we were leaving, Uncle Ted called out, "Bye-bye, see y'all later."

Palmer Lee called back, "Nice meeting you, Mr. Sizemore. Thanks for the Cherry Coke."

Walking back to The Quilt Shop, Palmer Lee said, "Can't wait to go to the pond with you and Wisteria. Sounds like fun. What time?"

"Be at my house at about one o'clock. By the way, my house is about a mile up the holler road. It's the white house on the right with the dark green shutters and a big porch with a red swing on it. Can't miss it. It has a huge sycamore tree in the front yard with a big, old black dog sleeping under it."

"Will I be safe from the big, old black dog?"

"Sure, but he might lick you to death—that is, if he wakes up—but that's about all he'll do."

"Okay, then, see you Saturday afternoon."

And I watched Palmer Lee turn and walk on down Main Street toward Miss Eulalee's bed and breakfast.

The bell rang when I walked through the door of The Quilt Shop. Wisteria was at the back of the store and glanced up when she heard the ding. When she saw that it was me, she looked away real quick and went on back to whatever it was she was doing.

When I reached her, I said, "Brought you a Cherry Co-Cola."

"Thanks. Just put it over there. I'll drink it later."

But she didn't drink it later. She didn't drink it at all. She let it sit there all day, till the ice was melted and her Cherry Co-Cola was all watered down. I knew she was just pouting and trying to let me know that she didn't like it one little bit that I was hanging out with Palmer Lee. I ignored her and went on back to work.

We were still working away silently, hadn't said one word to each other, when Mama said, "Time for you girls to head on out. You've had a long day."

Wisteria and I finished what we were working on and walked out together, but she was still quiet, with her head all hanging down.

"Wisteria, please don't be mad at me."

"I'm not mad, Bit. I'm just afraid."

"What are you afraid of?"

"I'm afraid you're gonna find somebody else and that you'll fire me as your best friend."

"Oh, Wisteria, please don't say that," I said, the tears starting in my eyes and me not caring if I looked like a damn sissy. "You'll always be my best friend, but I can have other friends, can't I, if I promise the others will never be my best?"

"Yeah, I guess so, but I can't compete with the likes of that purdy boy."

"It's not a competition, Wisteria. I like him, but not like I like you. But, you know, I'm getting of a certain age where I can start liking boys. And I kinda like Palmer Lee."

"I realize that, but knowing that about you is a hard pill to swallow."

Wisteria was forever saying stuff like that, and it was tough not to laugh at her. But she deserved not to be laughed at when she was hurting something awful.

"And one more thing, Wisteria. I've invited Palmer Lee to go up to the pond with us Saturday. And don't you say *damn*, you hear? He's all by himself up here, and he needs some friends. I think we ought to be his friends. I really want you to get to know him. He just might grow on you."

"I doubt that," she said, under her breath. Then she added, so that I could hear her perfectly well, "And, Bit, Saturday is our time."

"I know that, Wisteria. But he really wants to go."

She didn't answer.

"Well, I'll see you tomorrow," I said when we got to my house.

"Okay, bye," was all she said and headed off to her little rickety trailer down by the river with her head still hanging down and her hands crammed way deep in her overalls pockets.

EIGHT

Bit Just Wants
Everybody to Play Nice

When Saturday came, Palmer Lee knocked on my door at precisely one o'clock.

"You give great directions. Found your white house with the dark green shutters and the red porch swing so easy. Found the sycamore tree. Found the big black dog, sound asleep, when I came into the yard. I even went over and petted him a little, but he didn't wake up."

Palmer Lee was wearing one of those long, baggy bathing suits. This one was white, with red, blue, and yellow polka dots on it. Around his neck he had a blue beach towel with a palm tree on it. He wore brown leather flip-flops on his feet. He looked overdressed for the pond, but he looked so handsome to me.

"Told you. Come on in. Daddy's working today, and Buddy's helping him out, but Mama's in the kitchen. Come on in and say hey!"

I took him in the kitchen, and he said, "Hi, Mrs. Sizemore. It's strange not seeing you down at your store."

"It's strange not being there. I feel like I spend all my life in The Quilt Shop. It's good to be home, taking a break for a change, puttering around the house."

"Yes, ma'am, I'm sure. And thanks for letting me go swimming with Bit."

Mama had told me that it was nice of Wisteria and me to let Palmer Lee go to the pond with us. She said that he must be lonely, up here all by himself.

"Sure, Palmer Lee. I hope y'all have a good time," Mama said.

"Don't go away," I told Palmer Lee. "I gotta go get my towel."

And I ran to the linen closet to get my pink towel, the one I always take up to the pond. When I got back to the living room, I saw that Palmer Lee had wandered out of the kitchen and was looking at my piano.

"This is an awful pretty piano?"

"Yeah, it's an antique. It belonged to my Meemaw, and her grandmother before her."

"My mom would love this. She collects antiques. What kind of wood is that?"

"It's rosewood, and the flowers were all hand carved. I think it's beautiful too," I said, running my hand over my very own piano.

"Does your mom play?"

"A little."

"Your dad?"

"Ha, he couldn't find middle C if you put his finger on it."

"Then whose piano is it?"

"It's mine. I'm the one who plays the piano. Been playing for about eight years now."

"Wow! You must be good."

"Yep, you might say. I play for our school assemblies and the little kids' Sunday school classes. I even competed in the state piano competition over in Raleigh last year. Didn't win, but I did come in third."

"Wow, that's great!"

"Yeah, my teacher, Miss Mercy, says that's unheard of for a first-time competitor."

"Let me know when your next competition is. I'll come cheer you on."

I got kinda nervous, thinking about competing and having Palmer Lee watching me from the audience. But I told him I'd let him know.

Then he looked around and said, "Where's Wisteria? I thought she was going to the pond with us?"

"She is. But she called to say that she'd meet us up there. So we'd better go. I imagine she's already on the dock, pacing back and forth.

"Bye, Mama, see you later."

"Bye, Mrs. Sizemore," Palmer Lee called out.

Mama stuck her head out the kitchen door and said, "Bye, kiddos, y'all be careful, you hear?"

Mama thinks she's not doing her job if she doesn't say, "Be careful," every time me or Buddy goes out the door.

I started to go to the end of the porch and jump over the railing, which is the way I usually get off the porch to head up to the pond, but I decided that wouldn't be too ladylike. So I marched right down the steps and around the side of the house. Kitty—that's the crazy name Buddy gave our big old black dog—loves going up to the pond with me, but he didn't even stir from his nap when Palmer Lee and I walked by. So I just let him snooze.

Sure enough, Wisteria was already up at the pond, pacing up and down the dock. She was wearing a yellow two-piece bathing suit with her orange high-tops.

"I thought y'all would never get here."

"Well, Wisteria, Mama started giving orders, and you know..."

"Oh, yeah, then y'all are excused."

"Thanks, Wisteria, I figured you'd understand."

"But now that we're all here, last one in is a damn sissy!" Wisteria screamed. She kicked off her magic high-tops, ran to the end of the dock, and did a cannon ball into the pond. Her spindly little self hardly made a ripple.

Palmer Lee and I dropped our towels and stepped out of our sandals, and I said, "On your mark, get set, go!" and we both ran off the end of the dock, into the pond.

"Yeeeeeeeee!" Palmer Lee screamed when he came up for air. "This water is freezing!"

"Yeah, I suppose I should've warned you. It is a little chilly, but you'll get used to it before too long. This pond is fed by a mountain stream, and mountain streams are awful cold."

"No kidding!" he said, his teeth chattering, his lips already turning a little blue.

"And that stand of trees over there shields the water from the sun till mid-afternoon. But, like I said, swim around a bit, and you'll get used to it."

Sure enough, in just a few minutes, he was fine, just like I knew he'd be.

We laughed and splashed and dunked one other, but Wisteria wasn't her usual funny, happy-acting self. She didn't even have a joke for us.

"Where's my joke, Wisteria. Our friendship contract calls for a joke every time we get together."

"The day's not over. Give it time."

But I figured I wasn't gonna get my joke of the day. I guessed she was feeling that jealousy thing about me liking Palmer Lee and about her having to share our Saturday with him.

After a while I said, "I'm about swum out. I'm gonna sit on the dock in the sun for a while."

So I climbed out of the pond and watched as Palmer Lee and Wisteria swam and paddled around. First, he tried to talk to her, but she'd just ignore him and dunk under the water every time he opened his mouth. I think he just finally gave up and went his own way. And she went hers, which was in the opposite direction.

And I really wanted them to like each other.

"What's going on up here?" I heard someone ask and turned to see Buddy walking out on the dock with a towel in one hand and a paper sack in the other.

"Hey, I thought you were working with Daddy today."

"Yeah, I was, but he said I'd done such a great job, he'd let me go early," Buddy said and smiled and thumped me on the shoulder.

Wisteria and Palmer Lee had climbed out of the water and had joined us on the dock.

"Palmer Lee, this is by brother, Buddy."

"Good to meet you," Buddy said, and Palmer Lee said, "Same here."

"Hey, Cuteness, who you been cussing out lately?" Buddy asked Wisteria.

"Aw, Buddy, you know I don't cuss. I just quote."

"That's right. I forgot," Buddy said and laughed.

"Hey, Mama sent y'all some goin'-to-school cookies."

"Why do you call...?" Palmer Lee began to ask, and we all started laughing before he could finish.

"Well, when Buddy started kindergarten, he didn't want to go to school, so Mama bribed him into goin' by putting some of these cookies in his lunch sack."

Palmer Lee took a bite and said, "Yep, they could bribe me into going to school or doing just about anything. They're delicious."

"Then, eat up," Buddy said.

Wisteria munched on her cookie, but I noticed she was being awfully quiet, especially for Wisteria. I think Buddy could tell something wasn't quite right with her, so he leaned down and whispered in her ear. She looked up at him with a real sly grin.

"For sure," she said to him.

Then Buddy said to me and Palmer Lee, "Me and Cuteness here would like to challenge the two of you to a heated game of chicken. Who's up for it?"

"You in?" I asked Palmer Lee.

"Oh, I'm in," he said.

So I told Buddy, "Okay, Sizemore, you're on." And to Wisteria I said, "And you better bring your A-game, Jones!"

Then the four of us cannonballed into the pond, and Buddy and Palmer Lee swam to where they were about chest deep in the water. Wisteria and I swam over, and the guys squatted down low so we could climb onto their shoulders. Once we were situated, Wisteria and I hooked our toes behind Buddy and Palmer Lee's backs to keep us steady, and they grabbed ahold of our legs so we wouldn't tip off into the water. Then the guys walked up close together, so that Wisteria and I could grab hands.

"Let the battle begin!" Wisteria screamed.

Now, I could have flicked Wisteria off into the water with no trouble, but that wouldn't have been much fun at all. We wanted our duel to last, to make it look like a real contest.

We had been twirling around and pushing and pulling and squealing for a good long while when I felt a thump on my knee. I looked down to see Buddy giving me that old Sizemore eye squint. I knew what I had to do, so I squinted right back at my brother. The next time Wisteria gave me the slightest little nudge, I threw my hands in the air, squealed real loud, and toppled off into the water. When I came up for air, Wisteria was still sitting on Buddy's shoulders, pumping her fists in the air. And Buddy was strutting her all around, like Wisteria was king of the world.

When she had had her fill of gloating, she said, "Well, the victor needs to get on home. I promised Mama I'd be home in time to help her fix supper."

Buddy flipped her backward into the water, and she swam to the dock, climbed aboard, and jumped into her magic orange high-tops. She took one last goin'-to-school cookie out of the sack, grabbed her towel, and skipped on down the dock and up the path that would take her through the woods and down to the river and her rickety little trailer.

"I think I've had enough water for one day," I said and climbed onto the dock.

Buddy and Palmer Lee joined me.

"I don't believe Wisteria likes me too much," Palmer Lee said.

"Don't be too hard on Cuteness," Buddy told him. "She's a good kid. Cusses like a sailor, but she's harmless, doesn't aim her cussing at anybody in particular."

"And she's funny too," Palmer Lee said.

"She sure is. Just give her some time. She'll come around."

Palmer Lee stood up, grabbed his towel, and started drying off, saying, "I'd better be getting on back to town. We're going home tomorrow for a few days. Mama is in charge of some Junior League thing, but we'll be back Wednesday."

"Nice to meet you," Buddy said, standing up and socking his shoulder the way guys do. Palmer Lee socked him back. I can't figure out why guys do that. It looks awful goofy.

"Me too, Buddy. Thanks, Bit. I had fun."

"Sure, Palmer Lee. I'll see you when you get back."

When he was out of sight, Buddy sat down beside me and said, "He seems right nice."

"Yeah, I think he is."

"You like him a lot, don't you?"

"Yeah, I believe I do."

"Just be careful."

I wasn't quite sure what I needed to be careful about, so I just said, "Okay."

"And, Bit, don't let you liking Palmer Lee hurt Wisteria, you hear?"

"I'll try not to let it hurt her."

Then he reached in the cookie sack and said, "One left. I'll split it with you."

NINE

That Goose
Can Sing
the National Anthem?

Next day me, Mama, Daddy, and Buddy were pulling into our driveway on our way home from church when we saw Sheriff Roudebush and his deputy standing on our front porch. Sheriff was wearing his sunglasses, even though it was a cloudy day. I think he just liked the way he looked in sunglasses. He had his thumbs hooked in his belt loops, and he was chewing on a toothpick. His deputy, Jerry Bishop, was rocking back on his heels, looking at something on the toes of his boots. He wasn't wearing sunglasses. I believe Sheriff Roudebush didn't allow him to wear sunglasses because he didn't want his deputy looking as good as he did.

"What's going on, Sheriff?" Daddy asked when he stopped the car and climbed out.

"Got a call from Clement Sturges. Said Nita Rose's goose went missing last night."

I got out of the car and went over to chat with Sheriff Roudebush. I said, "You mean Larue?"

"Yep, that's the one."

"You suppose he escaped?" I asked. But after thinking about it, I added, "But why would he do that? He has about the easiest life I've ever seen for a goose. Why, he doesn't do anything but sing and wear that silly bandana."

"That's what we're trying to figure out, Bit."

Miss Nita Rose loves that goose like it's her very own child, seeing as how she doesn't have any real children. She has a different color bandana for each day of the week, and she'll wrap one of those colored things around Larue's neck every morning after he's finished with his breakfast. And that old goose will strut around in front of all the other geese, acting all high and mighty because he has a bandana and they don't. I figured maybe one of those other geese got jealous and shooed Larue off.

Miss Nita Rose swears that goose can sing the national anthem. Well, I've heard Larue sing, and, sure enough, he can make sounds other plain old honking geese can't make, but what he sings sure isn't the national anthem, leastwise not *our* country's national anthem. Maybe it's some other country's national anthem.

"What you reckon we can do about it, Sheriff?" Daddy asked. "Guess if a goose wants to wander off, it'll just wander off."

"Well, Harrison, I ain't said nothin' about it, but this ain't the first animal disappearance of late here in Lovington."

Daddy asked, "What do you mean not the first?"

"Well, last week Mayor Birdsong's prissy old dog, Lord Poodle, disappeared."

When Mayor Birdsong got that dog, I said to Wisteria, "Isn't naming a poodle dog Lord Poodle what you'd call ironic?

"No, Bit, that's what you'd call *moronic*. But I believe the word you're really looking for here is *redundant*."

"Wisteria, how do you know all this stuff?" I asked her.

"Well, Bit, I guess I'm just a walking thesaurus."

I figured I'd had enough lecturing from a twelve-year-old, so I decided to nip it in the bud and wait till I got home to look up the word redundant. And thesaurus.

But, anyway, the sheriff said that Lord Poodle had disappeared. "Mayor Birdsong opened his door to go down on Main Street to mingle with his constituents. Went back in to get hisself a linen hand-kerchief—because you know he don't go nowhere without a laundered and neatly pressed linen handkerchief—and when he returned, he found that Lord Poodle had slipped out. Ain't heard a yip from him since.

"Then shortly after Lord Poodle's disappearance, Miss Carrie's parakeet, Chirp, vanished from right out of his cage. Miss Carrie had hung Chirp's cage out in her back yard so that he could get some fresh air, and, poof, he just vanished."

"You suppose he flew away, Sheriff?"

"Nah, Harrison, Chirp had his wings clipped, just like Larue. So there's no chance them two flew the coop. I'm thinking we got our-selves a pet thief. That's what the pattern indicates."

"And you're here because...?"

"Well, Harrison, since you're on the town council, I thought you needed to be in the know."

"That's awful thoughtful of you, Sheriff. I'll keep my eyes peeled and my ears open. If I find any clues, I'll certainly let you know," Daddy said and sort of shook his head to clear the smirk that was forming on his face. I don't believe Daddy saw this as a crisis worthy of convening a special council meeting.

Just then Wisteria came flying down the holler road and into our yard. Her face was all red and sweaty, and she was breathing real hard. She leaned over and grabbed her side and took to panting.

Then she kinda wheezed, "What's going on? I heard when we were coming out of church that there'd been a kidnapping."

"It's Larue," I said. "Sheriff thinks somebody stole Larue."

"Well, I'll be d...arn," she said. "Who do you think would do such a thing, Sheriff Roudebush?"

"Could be anybody, Wisteria," the sheriff said, talking around the toothpick in his mouth. "Guess my biggest question is why? Who'd want a goose that purports to singing the national anthem?"

Wisteria had recovered from her run and piped up. "Well, that's a very good question. But I sure hope I'm not a suspect, 'cause I got me a solid alibi for my whereabouts."

"Wisteria," Sheriff Roudebush said, "you can't have an alibi when you don't even know when the crime took place. But, don't worry, you're not a suspect. We all know you wouldn't steal a goose, even a singing goose."

And Wisteria said, "Whew! That's good to know, 'cause I'm just too young to be doing hard time."

Then Sheriff Roudebush asked, "Harrison, you seen anybody suspicious wandering around up here?"

"Can't say that I have, Lonnie. But, like I said, we'll keep our eyes open. You think our pets are safe? Or should we pen 'em up?"

"Might not be a bad idea. Sure wouldn't want Kitty to turn up missing."

Walking toward his squad car with Jerry following close on his heels, Sheriff Roudebush said over his shoulder, "Just keep a watchful eye, Harrison, and give me a call if you see anything out of the ordinary."

"Will do, Sheriff."

I couldn't wait for Wednesday to come for Palmer Lee to get back from Raleigh so I could tell him about the excitement he'd missed while he was away. I'd told him that nothing exciting ever happened in our town, except for Bug's Jesus rock, and then Larue, Chirp, and Lord Poodle turn up missing, and Palmer Lee not even around to hear about it. But second-hand news is better than no news at all.

* * *

"You mean to tell me that your neighbor has a pet goose named Larue that sings the national anthem and wears a different colored bandana each day of the week?"

"Yes, Palmer Lee, but that's not the news part of the story. The news part is that somebody stole him."

"Why would somebody steal a goose?"

"Well, that's the mystery."

"Do they have any idea who did it?"

"None, but it could be just about anybody in Lovington, except Wisteria, 'cause she's got an alibi and has already been cleared."

"Well, that's good to know."

"Yes, she was quite relieved. Said she's just too young to serve hard time."

"I agree, but she'd look mighty good in one of those orange jumpsuits."

I play-slapped him on the arm and said, "Shame on you, Palmer Lee. Now, be nice to Wisteria."

"I'm just kidding, Bit. I know Wisteria wouldn't take somebody's pet. She just talks tough, right?"

"Yeah, but she's just quotin'." Then I added, "I didn't even ask about your trip. Did you have fun?"

"Well, it was good to be back in my own bed for a few days and to eat something for breakfast other than French toast casserole or cheese grits. But my mother's Junior League thing sure wasn't as exciting as what went on up here."

"What did you do while you were over in Raleigh?"

"Well, I played doubles with Cissie and Tandy and Trey at the club. Then we went to a movie and over to Char Grill for a Charburger. I guess that's about it. Then Mama and Daddy and I just came on back up here."

I was wondering what it would be like to play tennis at the club and go to a big-city movie theatre that shows brand new movies, instead of our Strand that shows hand-me-down movies that everybody else has already seen, and then go to our favorite hang-out for hamburgers. I was feeling kinda jealous of Cissie and Tandy and Trey because they got to do all those things with Palmer Lee. But I was feeling lucky at the same time. He had come on back to Lovington and wanted to spend time with me, even if I didn't know how to play tennis like his Raleigh friends.

While Palmer Lee and I were chatting, Wisteria came out of the stockroom on her way to the front of the store with an armload of quilts.

When she passed us, without even looking at us she said, "You two break it up. Bit needs to get back to work. Miss Brenda and Miss Nelda aren't paying her to chit-chat."

I wanted so bad to say something real sassy back to her, but, instead, I just told Palmer Lee, "Guess I better get back to work."

"Okay," he said, taking my hand. "Do you think I could come up to see you after supper tonight?"

Pulling my hand away because it made me feel self-conscious, I said, "I don't know. I'll have to ask my mama first."

He walked me up to the front of the store, and I asked, "Mama, could Palmer Lee come up to the house after supper tonight?"

She smiled and said, "Why, I think that would be fine."

"Thanks, Mrs. Sizemore. I'll see you later, Bit."

Watching him walk out the door and down Main Street, I craned my neck at the window and peered till I lost sight of him.

"I think it's nice that you're befriending Palmer Lee, seeing as how he doesn't have any friends up here. But break's over. Time to get back to stocking," Mama said, while I was still standing there, daydreaming about Palmer Lee coming up to see me.

When I got back to the stock room, Wisteria clamped her jaw down real tight and made slitty eyes at me. She huffed and pouted around, slinging quilts and dusting shelves like a woman on fire. I just let her because she was managing to do as much work by herself as the two of us usually did together.

When I got ready to leave for the afternoon, I said, "Come on, Wisteria, let's go home."

"You go on. I have a few more things to do here, and then I have to go down to the Piggly Wiggly to get something for Mama."

"Well, I'll help you finish up here, and then I'll walk down to the Piggly Wiggly with you."

"Nah," she said, "you go on."

There wasn't anything I could do to please her, except stop being friends with Palmer Lee. And I wasn't about to do that. She was just gonna have to get used to it, that's all.

TEN

A First Date
That's Really Not a Date

I walked on to the house by myself. Daddy and Buddy weren't home from work yet, and Mama wouldn't be home from The Quilt Shop for another thirty minutes or so, so I went ahead and set the table for supper. Mama had put the chicken in the Crock-Pot before leaving for work, and our supper was making the house smell so good. I opened the lid and stuck a fork in the chicken like Mama had showed me, and it felt all done to me. I turned off the cooker and went to my bedroom to find something special to wear when Palmer Lee came to visit later on.

I went through my drawers and found a denim skirt and a blue top that I liked real good. Mama said the top made my brown eyes stand out so pretty. Then I went rummaging in my closet and located one of my brown sandals. I found the other under my bed, behind my sixth-grade math book. I was certain I'd turned that thing back in to Miss Potter, the school librarian.

Then I went to the bathroom and drew me a bath. I even put in some of my lilac bubble bath that Buddy had gotten me for Christmas from Bath & Body Works over at the mall in Mount Pine. I didn't use it too often because I wanted it to last a long time. Then I pulled my hair up on top of my head and put a big clip on it before I climbed into the tub.

While I was bathing, I thought about how Wisteria was acting. I couldn't tell if it made me mad or sad. I didn't want to hurt her feelings, but she was hurting my feelings by not wanting me to act normal and grow up the way I was supposed to. Being so confused and all about the situation, I shook the thoughts out of my head and pondered about Palmer Lee instead.

"Bit, I'm home!" Mama yelled.

"Hey, Mama. I'm in the tub. I'll come help you with supper soon as I get out."

"I'm counting on it."

I pulled the plug, climbed out, and dried off real fast. I went to my bedroom and put on my Palmer Lee clothes and brushed my hair out real good. The sun was starting to make my sorta-blonde hair look like real-light-blonde hair. I liked my summer hair. People said it was pretty. Not Wisteria-Calliope-Jones-hair pretty, but pretty.

Just as I got to the kitchen, Daddy and Buddy walked in the back door and headed to the sink to wash their hands.

Mama had gotten supper just about ready without a lick of help from me.

She didn't complain, only said, "Just in time. Y'all sit down before everything gets cold."

When we sat down to eat, I draped a dish towel down the front of my shirt and tucked it in my collar.

"Why the bib, Itty Bitty?" Buddy asked.

"Just don't want to get my supper on my shirt."

"Special occasion?" Daddy asked. "You smell awful pretty, and you're wearing a mighty fine-looking outfit."

I blushed.

Mama said, "Senator Compton's son, Palmer Lee, is coming up to visit with Bit after supper."

I saw Daddy kinda cock his eyebrow, but before he could say anything, Mama said, "I told them it would be okay. Palmer Lee is all alone up here and could use a friend. He knows Bit's not allowed to date, but I didn't see any harm in having him up for a visit. Don't you agree, Harrison?"

I could tell that Mama was poking Daddy with her foot under the table.

"Well, I guess that would be all right, Bit, just as long as Palmer Lee knows that you're too young to date."

"Yes, Daddy, I understand. And Palmer Lee knows."

When I finished my supper, Mama said, "Bit, you run along and brush your teeth. I'll clean up here."

"Thank you, Mama," I said and ran off to get ready for Palmer Lee.

By the time I'd brushed my teeth, Palmer Lee was knocking at the door.

"Come on in, son. I'm Harrison Sizemore, Bit's father."

"Nice to meet you, Mr. Sizemore," I heard Palmer Lee say, and I knew he was shaking my daddy's hand like a grown-up. I was betting my daddy thought that was a polite thing for him to do.

I came out in the living room where Daddy and Palmer Lee were talking just as Mama came out of the kitchen.

"Hey, Palmer Lee. Could I get you something to drink. Ice tea? Co-Cola?"

"No, thank you, Mrs. Sizemore. We just had dinner down at Mr. Carl's. I'm fine for now."

"Well, I have some quilting to do, and Daddy has a town council meeting. Why don't y'all go on out to the swing?"

"Yes, ma'am," I said and led Palmer Lee out to the front porch.

We'd just sat down on the swing when Daddy came out and said, "See you kids later." Then he got in his truck and took off down the holler road.

"Where's Buddy?"

"He and Luke Jones went over to Mount Pine to shoot pool. Luke's Wisteria's big brother, and he and Buddy are good friends. So I'm afraid it's just you and me," I said, and I felt myself blushing.

Palmer Lee smiled and reached for my hand. "That's nice. Just you and me."

This time I didn't pull my hand away. I was still jittery, but I really wanted to hold hands with Palmer Lee.

As we swung back and forth, I said, "Tell me about Raleigh. I've only been over to the Capital on two field trips, one time to see the science museum and the other time to go to the governor's mansion. And, of course, there was the time I competed in the state piano competition. Everything seemed so big and busy and exciting. Is it exciting? And what do y'all do up there?" I asked, even though I'd already asked Palmer Lee about Raleigh before. But I wanted to hear it again.

"Well, Raleigh is a nice place. And, yeah, I guess you could say it's big and exciting, compared to Lovington. Not that Lovington's not nice," he said, sort of apologizing. "My friends and I mostly go to the club for fun. We swim and play tennis and golf. We go to the movie sometimes, and there's always a concert going on around Raleigh. And Mama and Daddy and I go to the club to eat with our friends. Of course, we have to do a lot of stuff for Daddy's political career, which I don't enjoy very much, but it's just something my mother has to do. Sometimes they drag me along."

"That sounds like lots of fun to me, meeting all those people, seeing all those pretty places. And going to concerts. I'd love to go to a music concert."

"Yeah, Raleigh is a good place to live, but this is awfully nice too. It's really peaceful out here. You can't hear the birds or see the stars in Raleigh the way you can out here. And listen," he said and got real quiet.

I listened real close, and then I said, "What? I don't hear anything."

"That's just it, you can't hear anything. No cars. No horns. No sirens. No airplanes. Maybe an occasional cricket or frog, but that's about it. Real nice."

Palmer Lee put his hand on my cheek, making me tingle way low in my tummy. Then he leaned in close and kissed me on the lips. It was the first time a boy had ever kissed me, unless you count the time me and Bucky Burns practice-kissed up at the pond when we were eleven years old.

Bucky had said to me, "Well, we gotta be prepared, don't we, for when the real thing happens?"

I thought that had made a whole lot of sense, so I went along.

We'd banged our noses together and he'd pressed his lips against mine real hard. His lips were chapped and dry, and I'd decided that if that was all there was to kissing, then it wasn't anything special.

But kissing Palmer Lee was special, and very different from kissing Bucky Burns. Palmer Lee was careful not to bang noses with me, and his lips weren't at all dry and chapped. They was real soft and kinda wet, and he stayed with his lips on my lips for a good, long while.

"I've wanted to do that for a good while, Bit," he said when he took his lips away from mine.

"Me too," I said, but I really didn't know I had wanted Palmer Lee to kiss me until he'd done it.

Then he put his arm around my shoulders and pulled me close to him, and he kissed me again, this time even longer than the first time.

I asked Palmer Lee, "Would you like to walk up to the pond?"

"Sure."

"Well, first I gotta see if Mama will let me go," and I went to the door and yelled, "Mama, can me and Palmer Lee walk up to the pond?"

"Sure, but you be back by dark, you hear?"

"Yes, ma'am," I called and motioned for Palmer Lee to come on.

Soon as we were out of sight of the house, Palmer Lee put his arm around my shoulders, and I put my arm around his waist. I had seen boys and girls in the movies walk like that, and I wanted to see how it felt. And I liked the way it felt. We walked like that all the way till we got up to the pond.

"I love this place, Bit. You wouldn't find anything this peaceful and pretty in Raleigh."

"Good," I said, and I was glad we had something that Raleigh didn't have. I wanted Palmer Lee to want to leave Raleigh and Cissie and Tandy and Trey and come up to see me.

We walked out to the end of the dock and sat down. We weren't there long before Palmer Lee started kissing me again, and this time we kissed and kissed for a real long time, till I said, "I better be getting on home. Looks like it's getting dark, and Mama'll start to worry if we're out too late."

"Okay, but I really don't want to go."

"I know. Me neither."

But we got up and put our arms around each other again, like the boys and girls in the movies, and walked on back to my house, our hips rubbing against each other. When we got home, we saw that Daddy's car was in the drive. He was back home from his meeting.

Palmer Lee walked me up on the porch and kissed me one last time and said, "Night, Bit. I had a good time."

"Me too," I said, and watched him stick his hands in the pockets of his shorts and walk on out the yard and down the holler road.

When I went inside, I saw Mama and Daddy watching TV.

"Did you and Palmer Lee have a nice time?" Mama asked.

"Yes, ma'am. He really likes it up at the pond. Said there isn't anything in Raleigh so pretty and peaceful."

"That's nice," Mama said and looked back at the TV and laughed at something. Daddy laughed too.

"I think I'll go to my room and read."

"Okay, darling, I'll come in and kiss you good-night before I go to bed," Mama said.

"Night-night, Bit," Daddy called after me.

I dropped my clothes on my chair and kicked my sandals under the bed. Then I put on my pajamas and picked up *The Outsiders*, one of the books I'd checked out at the library the week before. I climbed into bed, propped my pillow against the headboard, and opened the book to where I'd left off the last time.

But I couldn't concentrate on reading. All I could think about was Palmer Lee. I touched my lips. They felt like they should be all puffy and red from the kissing we'd done. I closed my book and slid out of bed. I looked in the mirror above my dresser. I was really surprised when I saw that my lips looked normal because I didn't feel normal.

ELEVEN

Squirrel in Cream Gravy at the Joneses' Respectable Three-Bedroom, One-and-One-Half Bath Brick Ranch-Style House

"Well, Bit, Mama says now that we're settled in our new house, you can come for supper. It's high time I started paying you back for all those Piscopal potlucks. I know it's been a dang long time, but it seems like it takes a man about forever to build his family a respectable house, especially when he's doing it all by himself and he has another job, to boot. But Mama has set aside Thursday evening as the time for the first supper. Course, we're having squirrel with cream gravy on rice, just like I promised we would. I want your first time to be real special."

"Thanks, Wisteria, that'll be so nice."

I could still feel the hurt coming off Wisteria whenever Palmer Lee was around. I was torn, but I was liking Palmer Lee more and more, and I didn't think it was fair that Wisteria didn't want me to like him. But, as she said, she was scared, and she still didn't think she could compete with a big-city purdy boy.

But Wisteria's daddy had built her family a brand new, three-bed-room, one-and-one-half bath, brick ranch-style house, and she was so excited about showing it to me. What's more, she was going to have me all to herself.

When Thursday evening came, I put on clean jeans and a fresh shirt and pulled my hair back into a ponytail. I even put on some fresh deodorant and brushed my teeth.

"Mama, I'm leaving for Wisteria's," I said, when I came into the kitchen to kiss her good-bye.

"Here, sweetie, take these cookies and this candle to Faylene, and tell her to let me know when she's good and settled, so I can pay her a visit to see her new house."

Mama always takes goin'-to-school cookies when she goes visiting or gives them to Buddy and me when we go to somebody's house for a special occasion. She got the candle over in Mount Pine when she and I went over to the craft shop to get some stencils to make signs for The Quilt Shop. The candle was red, and the label said it smelled like apples and cinnamon, like a fresh-baked apple pie. Mama thought it would be a real nice addition to Miss Faylene's kitchen.

"I will, Mama," I said, taking the sack of cookies and the candle that she had wrapped in pink-striped tissue paper.

"Now, you be real polite and help Faylene with the dishes, you hear?"

"Yes, ma'am."

Mama always tells me to be polite and help with the dishes. I bet she'll be telling me that when I'm sixty years old.

I walked up the holler road, and when I got to Wisteria's house, I found her sitting on the front stoop, waiting for me. When she saw me come around the bend, her face lit up, like she hadn't seen me just an hour before.

"Hey, Wisteria," I called out and waved when I came into the yard. She jumped up and ran to meet me.

"Come on in. I can't wait to show you our new house. And everybody's so glad you're coming for supper."

"Me too."

Wisteria led me in the front door and said, "This here is the living room," spreading her arms like she was presenting a prize on *Let's Make a Deal.*

"This is real pretty, Wisteria."

"Yeah, I know. And if you'll follow me this way, I will show you the three bedrooms and the one-and-one-half bathrooms."

First she showed me the one-half bathroom right off the living room. It was little, but it had all the things a one-half bathroom needed to have. Then we came to Earl, Jr. and Luke's bedroom. It looked just like Buddy's bedroom to me, with two twin beds and a dresser to match and tennis shoes and a basketball and jackets on the floor. Next Wisteria showed me Miss Faylene and Mr. Earl's bedroom. It was real nice. Miss Faylene had decorated it so pretty, with frilly green checked curtains and some ruffly green throw pillows on the bed. There was a cute little dressing table with a three-way mirror, like the ones you see in old-timey movies, with a round, green tufted stool to go with it. So far, this was my favorite room. Then Wisteria took me to her and Faye's and Virginia's room. There were three twin beds, but I guess since there were three, that would make them triplet beds. They were all lined up, side by side by side with yellow flowered bedspreads, and the walls were painted a real bright yellow. I could tell that Daddy Earl had let Wisteria pick out the paint since yellow is her favorite color—after orange, of course.

"This is so pretty, Wisteria."

"I know. I had a hand in decorating it."

"I can tell. You did a great job."

"And over here, across the hall, is our big bathroom."

It didn't look much different from any other bathroom I'd ever seen, except it had a whole bunch of towel bars with towels hanging on them, since the Joneses have seven people in their family. But I told Wisteria that it was very nice and that I bet she liked taking a bath in her new bathtub, since she'd told me there was just a tiny little shower in Papa Luke's rickety little trailer down by the river. She said she did like it very much.

The rest of the house was one big room, with the dining room and kitchen blending all together.

When we got to the kitchen, Wisteria said, "Hold it right there. I'll be back directly." And then she ran out the back door.

Miss Faylene was standing at the stove, cooking. "Hey, Bit, I'm glad you could join us for supper."

"Thanks, Miss Faylene, it was awful nice of you to invite me. I like your new house. It's real pretty."

"Thank you so much. I think we're going to like spreading out. That trailer was getting mighty cramped."

"Here, Miss Faylene," I said, handing her the sack of cookies and the candle in the pink-striped tissue paper. "Mama asked me to bring these to you."

"Thank you so much, Bit. Just put them right there on the counter. I'll look at them after I finish fixing supper. By the way, Bit, I hope you like squirrel."

"I like fried squirrel, Miss Faylene, but I haven't ever had squirrel fixed with cream gravy. But I'm sure I will like it. Wisteria loves it, and that's a good enough advertisement for me."

Just then Miss Faylene yelled, and I jumped in astonishment.

"Wisteria, get that thing out of my kitchen right now! You know it doesn't belong in this house!"

I turned around, and right there in Miss Faylene's kitchen was a little white goat, hopping around and dancing and clicking its tiny hooves on the tiled floor.

Ignoring her mama for the time being, Wisteria said, "Well, Bit, what'cha think?"

"I think it's real cute, especially the way it tap dances around on its tip-toes like that. But where'd you get a goat?"

But when Miss Faylene turned around from the stove and scowled real hard and pointed her wooden cooking spoon at Wisteria, she said, "Come on, Bit, let's get her out of here before Mama has a conniption."

Wisteria picked up the little goat, and its hooves just kept on tap dancing in midair. I followed her out the kitchen door toward the shed Mr. Earl had built out in the back yard.

"Like I asked, Wisteria, where'd you get a goat, and how come I haven't ever heard about it?"

"Well, Daddy Earl just now got it for me. He said everybody's got somebody but me, so he figured I deserved a body too. You know, Faye and Virginia have each other. Luke and Earl, Jr. have each other. Mama and Daddy's got each other. Now me and my goat's got each other," she said and kissed the thing on the nose while it just kept on dancing in the air.

"Why a goat? Why not a dog or a cat?"

"Well, Bit, I asked the very same thing. Daddy Earl said, 'A dog and a cat are just so ordinary. And there's nothing ordinary about my Wisteria.'"

"Gotta say I agree with Mr. Earl on that one. I guess a baby goat is a perfect pet for you."

"Thanks. I was hoping you'd like her."

"What's her name?" I asked, reaching over to pat the little thing on its head.

"NaCl," she said.

"'Scuse me?"

"NaCl," she said again.

"How do you spell that?"

"Capital N, little A, capital C, little L, just like it sounds."

"Where'd you get a name like that?"

"Well, I was reading Luke's chemistry book...," she started.

"Just for fun?" I asked.

"Well, more out of curiosity than for fun. Turns out it wasn't much fun a'tall. But it did satisfy my curiosity. And I came across this name, NaCl, and I figured that sounded like a good name for a pygmy goat."

"Can't say I ever heard of that one."

"Guess that's 'cause you're not a student of chemistry."

"Well, yeah, I guess not."

"Turns out, though, NaCl wasn't such a good name, after all."

"Why's that?"

"Well, Luke says to me, 'Why'd you name your goat Sodium Chloride?' And I said, 'Didn't name her any such thing. I named her NaCl.' Then Luke says, 'Same thing. Na stands for the element sodium, and Cl stands for the element chloride. Put 'em together, you got sodium chloride. And, Wisteria, sodium chloride is just another name for salt. So you've really named your goat Salt.' So I said, 'You're overthinking it, Luke. I just named her NaCl. Okay?' Luke finally said it sounded like a cool name. But just like Buddy naming your dog Kitty, what difference does it make, as long as you feed 'em real good and pet 'em a lot and say 'Good boy!', or, in this case, 'Good girl!', every chance you get?"

"Guess you're right, Wisteria."

Wisteria carried NaCl on out to the shed and took her into a little pen off to one side. She sat down and said, "Lay down, NaCl. That's a good girl."

Wisteria held NaCl close and petted her real soft and hummed to her. Then she got up and locked her goat in her pen.

Then she said to me, "She's a real good hanging-on-to friend. Now let's go eat some squirrel with cream gravy."

Eating supper at the Joneses' house was real loud with words that ricocheted against one another like bumper cars. I guess that's what it's like when you have seven people in your family, everybody talking at once, trying to be heard above the rest, trying to make sure everybody is happy with one another, and nobody wants anybody else to be up to no good.

I was eating along, minding my own business, dodging all those loud words, when Luke said, "Earl, Jr., pass me a roll."

Instead of passing Luke the entire bread basket, like we do at our house, Earl, Jr. just up and threw a roll at his brother from one end of the table to the other. Luke caught it, mid air, smeared some butter on it, and started eating it, like nothing out of the ordinary had just happened. I couldn't believe my eyes, but not another soul paid any attention or stopped eating or talking or sent anybody to his bedroom to think about his behavior. Which is exactly what would've happened if Buddy ever threw a roll at me at the supper table.

And one other thing about eating supper with the Joneses: Squirrel with cream gravy ain't all it's cracked up to be. Maybe it'll grow on me, but I have my doubts.

TWELVE

Bleeding the
Sorrow Out

Once we'd finished our supper, I was slap worn out from all the backin' and forthin' and the food throwing from that big old Jones family, so I was ever so relieved when Wisteria said, "Let's go out back and lay on the trampoline and let our supper settle."

"Well, let's help your mama with the supper dishes first."

"Nah, tonight's Faye and Virginia's turn to help. Anyway, you're company. You don't have to help."

So I said, "Thank you for the squirrel with cream gravy, Miss Faylene. That was awful good."

I wasn't perfectly honest, but I was perfectly polite.

"You're welcome, Bit. Now, you girls run along and have a fun time."

We went out in the Jones's back yard, but I was so full it was hard to hoist myself up on the trampoline. Once I did, though, I just lay on my back so everything could settle, like Wisteria had suggested. Wisteria shimmied her skinny little self up with no trouble at all and scooted over close to me, crossed her legs, and started concentrating on the scab on her knee. I hadn't seen Wisteria fall and skin her knee a single time since she'd become my best friend forever, but she always seemed to have a scab to worry with.

I guess Mama was right when she said, "If you worry a scab, it'll never heal."

And I noticed she worried with it most when she had something serious to say and just didn't want to look me in the eye.

So I prepared myself for some serious Wisteria talk. I folded my arms behind my head and peered up at the sky that was coming on to night.

"Bit, there were several reasons I invited you to supper tonight. First off, I was real anxious for you to see my new respectable home. I hope you like it."

"Oh, Wisteria, I sure do. It's beautiful. Your daddy did an excellent job making a nice home for you and your family."

"Thank you. I was quite certain you'd feel that way. Second, I wanted you to taste my mama's squirrel with cream gravy. Good, isn't it?"

Once again, I was polite, if not completely honest. "Sure is, just like you told me."

"And, of course, you needed to become acquainted with NaCl."

"Of course."

"But there's another thing, Bit."

"What's that, Wisteria?"

"Well, I learned something recently that I failed to uncover in my research, and it's troubling me something awful."

I froze. Without Wisteria telling me, I knew what she was talking about. She and I pretty much told each other everything, seeing as how we were best friends and all, but I had been harboring a big secret from her. I was pretty sure my secret would ooze out at some time or another, but I wasn't ready for it to ooze just yet, wasn't ready to talk about it, would never really be ready to talk about it. So I decided never to speak of it and to let it come to light at its own pace.

"What's that?" I said, all casual-like.

"You had a sister I didn't know about."

There it was. My secret. My secret that hurt so bad I could hardly catch my breath every time I thought about it. Sondra had been gone four years. But it still hurt like it had just happened. I felt like it would hurt forever and ever like it had just happened. I didn't want to talk about it, didn't want Wisteria to ask me about it. But she was my best friend, and best friends don't keep secrets. Even the hurting kind.

"I'm sorry I didn't know, Bit."

"That's okay, Wisteria."

"No, it's not. Best friends ought to know these things."

"But I didn't tell you."

She waited a long time, concentrating on her knee. Finally, without looking at me, she said, "Will you tell me now?"

I took a really, really deep breath and held it there for a long time. Then when I thought I might be able to say Sondra's name and breathe at the same time, I said, "Okay."

I really didn't know where to start. But Wisteria kept her yap shut, for a change, and let me figure it out in my time.

"Her name was Sondra. She was my best friend. Before Naomi June Lockleer. Before you."

I could feel my heart racing and the cry lump starting in my throat. I waited for them to go away.

I took another deep breath and said, "Every day for a long time after she died, I'd wake up and I'd either be sad or mad. I knew why I was sad, but I just couldn't figure out the mad part. Maybe I was just mad that there were some people left here on earth and Sondra wasn't one of them. Trouble was I didn't know which I was gonna be—mad or sad—till the time came. I told Mama how I was feeling, and she said, 'It's okay to be mad and sad, but we'd rather have Sondra in heaven than still suffering here on earth.' Don't know if I agree with that, though, Wisteria, 'cause I was never consulted on the matter, and I sure didn't get a vote!"

Wisteria shook her head in that knowing way of hers, like she could feel what it felt like to be me.

"Why'd she die?"

"Weak heart. She was born with a weak heart. Mama and Daddy and the doctors tried everything they knew how to do. They took her to specialists at Duke Hospital, over in Durham, but nothing they did for her seemed to work."

"That's sad."

"Yeah."

Me and Wisteria lay there in silence for a long time, looking up at the sky, listening to the coming-on-to-night sounds of crickets and bullfrogs.

Finally Wisteria broke the silence when she said, "What was she like?"

"She was pretty, lots prettier than me. She had long, golden blonde hair and great big green eyes, like Daddy's. I can't look into Daddy's eyes and not think about Sondra," I said and had to stop for a minute to push the cry lump back down. "And she was smart, smart like Wisteria Calliope Jones smart."

"Real smart, huh?"

"Yeah, real smart. Fact is, she was your age. And she had skipped a grade too. She'd have been in your class."

"Is that why you let me be your best friend?"

"No, Wisteria, I wanted you to be my best friend because of you, not because of Sondra."

"What kind of stuff did she like to do?" Wisteria asked.

"She loved birds and knew just about everything there was to know about birds. She was just a little girl, but she was already planning to go to college and study to be an ornithologist. That's somebody who knows stuff about birds."

"I know what an ornithologist is, Bit," Wisteria said, cutting her eyes sideways at me.

"I figured you did, Wisteria."

"Did Sondra give you that bird's nest you've got sitting on your desk in your bedroom?"

"Yeah, her last Christmas she was my secret Santa. That bird's nest was a secret Santa gift. Course, soon as I saw the bird's nest, my Santa wasn't a secret anymore."

"That's nice."

"And, Wisteria, she was funny as all get-out."

"Funnier than me?"

"Sometimes," I said. "She'd be funniest when she wasn't supposed to be, like when we were meant to be sleeping. We'd be laying in that big, old feather bed in my room, and she'd start to cuttin' the fool. I'd begin to laughing, and Daddy'd call out, 'Bit, don't make me come in there.' I think Daddy knew all along it was Sondra who put me up to giggling, 'cause he knew how funny she was. But I believe he didn't like scolding Sondra. Didn't any of us like scolding Sondra. I guess we figured her sickness had given her about all the scolding a little body could handle."

"I bet that was a sad time for Miss Brenda and Mr. Harrison. Mamas and daddies ought not to have their babies die."

"Yeah, they were real sad. During the day, though, Mama was so brave. I guess she didn't want me and Buddy to see her break down. But at night I'd hear her crying in her and Daddy's bed, real sad. Just about broke my heart. And I'd hear my sweet daddy saying to her, 'There, there, Bren.' I believe he was trying to make her stop crying. And, Wisteria, I disagree with you about crying making you a damn sissy. I think that if your heart is heavy with sorrow, you ought to cry and cry and cry till the sorrow bleeds right out."

"Is that what you did when Sondra died?"

"Yeah."

"Did it work?"

"For a while. You see, I think that when you cry and cry and cry out the sorrow, even a little of that sorrow will hide from you, and then when you're least expecting it, it'll seep back in and cause some more pain to well up. Then you have to cry that sorrow out. Course, you don't ever really get rid of all the sorrow. But it can hide for just so long. The more you cry, the weaker it gets, till you have just enough sorrow left over so you never, ever forget what made you sorrowful in the first place."

"Makes sense," she said, and I could tell she was giving it some serious thought. "Hearing about your sister dying makes me feel guilty."

"But why, Wisteria? You didn't have anything to do with it."

"I know I didn't, but I'm always talking about my problems. They don't feel like anything compared to having a baby sister die. Faye and Virginia can be pains in the be-hind, but I can't imagine how sad I would be if one of them died."

"It is sad, Wisteria, but just 'cause your sister didn't die doesn't mean your sorrows aren't real. Everybody's got sorrows, and no matter what kind of sorrows they are, they're still your sorrows, and they make you hurt in a real big way."

I could tell by the look on Wisteria's face that some of her sorrow was seeping into her heart. But she refused to cry. She still wasn't quite believing that crying wouldn't make her a damn sissy.

"I gotta get on home, Wisteria. Mama doesn't want me walking the holler road by myself after dark," I said.

Truth be told, some sorrow had seeped into my heart, too, and I needed to bleed it out by myself.

Wisteria scooted off the trampoline and reached up to take my hand and help me down to the ground.

She stood on her tip-toes and put her arms around my neck, giving me a hug. "I'm so glad you're my best friend."

I hugged her back and said, "Same here, Wisteria," 'cause that was about all I had left in me.

I walked real slow, and some of my sorrow bled out on my way home. When I got to our yard, I mopped my face with my sleeve 'cause I didn't want Mama to see me crying and ask me why. It helped my heart a lot when I saw Mama through the kitchen window. When she saw me coming across the yard, she smiled and waved. My mama's smile has a way of tamping down the saddest of sorrows.

THIRTEEN

Jesus Take
the Wheel

Once Wisteria got settled in her new house, we spent lots of time hanging out at her place. It was one spot she figured she could compete with Palmer Lee because he just had one room at Miss Eulalee's B&B, and she had a whole respectable, brick ranch-style home. And when we were at her house, I was hers and hers alone.

One afternoon after work we'd walked up to her house, and we were laying on our backs on her trampoline, naming the clouds.

"They all look like sheep to you, Bit. Don't you have any imagination a'tall? Now, look close at that one. That's a dragon. See?"

I didn't see. It looked like a sheep to me.

"There. Right there," Wisteria said, leaning in so her pointing arm was right by my left eye, "that wispy cloud. That's the smoke coming out of the fire-breathing dragon's nostrils. See?"

I didn't see, but I knew she wouldn't let up till I said she was right and that I could see her dragon with the smoke coming out of his nostrils.

"Oh, yeah, a dragon. I see it now."

"Damn right."

"Just quotin'?"

"Course. I always quote."

That's when we heard it, heard it through Miss Faylene's open kitchen window.

"Please don't, Earl."

"Stop nagging at me, Faylene."

"But, Earl, I can't bear it anymore."

Then Miss Faylene started crying.

That's when Wisteria started naming all the clouds real fast. "That's a bunny. See his long ears? The left one is flopping a bit. And that's just a snake. He's coiled and ready to strike. His forked tongue is sticking out. And that's either a possum or a badger, can't tell those two apart."

She talked loud and she talked fast, filling up all the dead air so her mama's tears couldn't seep into the cracks. But they managed to seep in anyway, and we could hear Mr. Earl's angry words and Miss Faylene's crying.

Finally, Wisteria stopped chattering and sighed from the weight of it all. It's hard for a little girl to try to keep her daddy from wanting to be up to no good and to keep her mama from crying about it.

So I said, "Mama's fixing a ham with pineapple rings for supper."

"You think she'd have enough for me?" Wisteria asked without looking at me.

"Wisteria, Mama's always got enough ham with pineapple rings for you. Or anything else, for that matter."

Mama doesn't like for us to invite friends to supper without asking her first, but she makes an exception for Wisteria. Mama's come to know her home situation, and if suppers and sleep-overs will ease her sorrow, Mama is happy to oblige.

"Go get your pajamas and ask Miss Faylene if you can eat supper at my house and sleep over with me. Okay?"

"Okay," she said, wiggling to the edge of the trampoline and dropping down on the ground.

I stayed put on the trampoline because I didn't want to see Miss Faylene crying, didn't want to lay eyes on Mr. Earl and his hurtful ways.

Wisteria came back out in about five minutes, her yellow ruffly shorty pajamas in one hand, her toothbrush in the other.

"Mama says I can go but I gotta be back early in the morning."

"Why's that?"

"'Cause we gotta go downtown to Mr. Simpson's photography studio to get our family picture took for the Baptist Church directory."

"That's fine, Wisteria. We'll get Daddy to wake us up early."

"Bit, I know that Saturdays are supposed to be for me and you to work on our friendship, but this is for family, you know. And I'm a big part of this family."

I just smiled at the little girl who wanted to believe that she could be a part of a big, loving, normal family and said, "Of course, Wisteria, I understand."

"I figured you would, Bit."

We walked down the holler road to my house, Wisteria swinging her pajamas by the straps, the ruffled bottom dragging in the dust. She either didn't notice or didn't care. I didn't say a word. I figured if dragging her pajamas in the dust brought her some sort of comfort, I'd just let her be.

When we came into the yard, we saw Kitty sound asleep under his sycamore tree. Normally Wisteria would wake him up and chuck him under the chin and kiss him on the nose. This time, though, she just walked on by, her head all hanging down, her pajama ruffle still dragging on the ground.

Mama was just taking the ham out of the oven when we walked in the back door.

"Hey, girls," she said. "Wisteria, it looks like you've come to stay."

"Mama, Wisteria's gonna eat supper and spend the night. That's okay, isn't it?" I said and squinched up my eyes at her, giving her that signal of ours that says something is up and you just need to play along.

"Why, certainly, it's okay," Mama said and wiped her hands on her apron and came over and put her arm around Wisteria and gave her a little squeeze.

Then she said, "Now, you girls go put Wisteria's pajamas in your room and wash your hands. I could use some help setting the table."

"Yes, ma'am," we both said.

Once we'd washed our hands, we headed back to the kitchen to help Mama. Wisteria knew where the dishes and forks were, so she went to setting the table all by herself. I just let her be.

When Mama started putting the food on the table, she said, "Bit, go out back and call Daddy and Buddy to supper."

My daddy and my brother were up digging in the vegetable garden, so I yelled real loud, "Y'all, supper's ready!"

They looked my way and waved in the air, letting me know they'd heard me calling. They both pulled their bandanas out of their back pockets and wiped their faces and headed down the hill, toting their hoes. I waited on the porch for them to put their tools in the shed.

When they got to the house, I said, "Hey, y'all."

Buddy said, "Hey, Itty Bitty," and Daddy kissed me on the top of my head and said, "How's my best girl?"

"I'm fine, Daddy. And Wisteria's eating supper with us."

"Great! Wisteria's always good for a laugh," Daddy said.

Daddy and Buddy dropped their muddy boots by the back door and headed for the kitchen sink, crowding each other to wash up for supper. They dried their hands on the towel Mama had special for them so they wouldn't use her dish towel for hand drying.

Buddy sat down beside me, reached over and tugged Wisteria's orange braid, and said, "How you been, Cuteness? Haven't seen you in ages."

"Oh, just been working, you know," Wisteria said and, cocking her head in Mama's direction, added, "'cause our boss drives us real hard."

Course, Daddy and Buddy laughed, never suspecting there was a single thing out of kilter in Wisteria's life.

Buddy asked her, "Heard any good jokes lately?"

"Hmmm," she said, "hold on and let me think."

She closed her eyes for a spell and then said, "What's the sound porcupines make when they kiss?"

When none of us could come up with the answer, she said, "Ouch!"

We all laughed. The joke was funny but not nearly as funny as Wisteria.

After supper I said, "Wisteria, why don't you go on and take your bath, and I'll help Mama clean up the supper dishes."

"Can I use some of your lavender bubble bath?"

"Sure," I said, as she took off for the bathroom.

Me and Mama were standing side-by-side at the kitchen sink, her rinsing, me loading the dishes in the dishwasher when I asked, "Mama, has Daddy ever been up to no good?"

When I said that, Mama stopped her rinsing and looked at me real hard and said, "No, honey. You have a good daddy. He loves me, and he loves you and Buddy. You don't have a thing to worry about."

"Wisteria says Mr. Earl is up to no good. What exactly does being up to no good mean?"

"Well, it can mean a lot of things, Bit, but, mostly, I guess it means you don't treat your family as nice as you ought to."

"He makes Miss Faylene cry, and there's nothing Wisteria hates worse than crying."

"Damn sissy?" my mama said, knowing that Wisteria cusses but figuring she has a reason.

"Yeah, but she's not cussing, just quoting."

"I understand," Mama said and chuckled.

When me and Mama finished with the supper dishes, she dried her hands and put her arms around me real tight and said, "You are my heartstrings, Bit. And you're your daddy's heartstrings too. We'll always love you and Buddy."

"I know, Mama," I said and went to see if Wisteria had turned into a prune.

When I came down the hall, I could hear her splashing around in the tub, singing, "Jesus take the whee-ee-eel," a song I'd heard Miss Faylene singing many a time.

When I got to the bathroom, I saw that Wisteria had filled up the tub near about to the very top, just her head sticking out of the water. She had unbraided her beautiful orange hair, and it was spread all out and floating on top. She had a pile of shampoo bubbles on top of her head.

When she saw me come around the corner, she quit singing and broke into a big grin. "I figured I'd better wash my hair if we're having our Baptist Church directory picture took tomorrow down at Mr. Simpson's. What'cha think of my bubble hat? Awesome, huh?"

Before I could answer, she lathered her hair up good, took a real deep breath, and disappeared underneath the water. When she came back up, she'd washed the shampoo out of her hair and was ready to get out.

"I'll go put on my pajamas," she said, drying off real fast. "Then I'll come sit on the pot and keep you company while you're taking your bath. Then you can dry my hair with your hair dryer. Okay?"

"Sure, Wisteria, that sounds fine."

When she left, I scrubbed her ring out of the tub and was draining the water when she came back in wearing her dusty, yellow pajamas. Her long, orange hair was wet and dripping down her back. She sat down on the toilet while I filled the tub back up and undressed and dropped my clothes in the hamper.

She pulled up her pajama top and poked herself in the chest and said, "How come I don't got any boobs yet? You said if I ate fried chicken at the Piscopal potluck, I'd get me some boobs. I'm going on twelve and five-eighths years old, and I'm still flat as a pancake. And you're just about popping out of your Double-A's. Doesn't seem fair."

"Well, Wisteria, I'm almost fifteen. I should have boobs. Give it time. You'll get some too."

Still poking at her flat little chest, she said, "Yeah, and when I do, I'm gonna get me a boyfriend."

"Wisteria, you won't need boobs to get you a boyfriend. You're gonna get a boyfriend with your brain."

Yanking down her pajama top, she said, "Damn right!"

Climbing into the tub, I looked back over my shoulder at her and said, "You've been quotin' an awful lot lately."

She smiled real big, showing me her tooth gap. "Got a whole lot to quote about," she said.

After I'd taken my bath and dried off and put on my pajamas, I said, "Okay, come on over to my bedroom, and I'll dry your hair."

She followed me and sat down at my dressing table, her feet swinging back and forth.

I combed her long hair out straight, all the way past her waist, and was drying it with my hair dryer when she said, "Can I sleep with Katy Perry tonight?"

Katy Perry is one of the many stuffies—that's my name for stuffed animals—that Buddy has won for me over the years at the shooting gallery at the Fall Is Just Around the Corner Festival. So far he's gotten me a panda bear, two teddy bears, a chicken with real feathers, a pink pig, and a little brown horse with a leatherette saddle with red and blue rhinestones on it. But the Katy Perry Wisteria was referring to is a big, long green furry snake. And I don't like snakes. Not one little bit.

But when Buddy won it for me, he said, "See, Itty Bitty, it can't hurt you. It's just made out of fur, and it has long eyelashes. It's even smiling."

Didn't matter if it did have long eyelashes and a smile, I still didn't like the thing. But I figured if I named it something pretty, like Katy Perry, that might change my mind about it. But I was wrong. It was a reminder of a scary time, and it still gave me the willies. So I just put it up on my shelf that Daddy had built me just for my stuffies and stuck all the rest of my stuffies in front of it so I wouldn't remember.

But Wisteria loved the dang thing and was wanting to sleep with it. In my bed!

"Wisteria, you know I don't want it in the bed with me."

"I promise I won't let her touch you. Promise! Promise!"

"Okay, Wisteria, you keep it on your side of the bed, and you can sleep with it. But you better not let it touch me in the night."

"I just said I won't."

"Okay, it's a deal."

Then she said, "You never told me why you don't like Katy Perry."

"No, I never did."

"Will you tell me now?"

"Well, it's 'cause I'm really afraid of snakes."

"That's understandable, Bit, but Katy Perry is not a real snake, you know."

"Of course I know, Wisteria. But it reminds me of a real snake and a real scary time, and I just don't like to think of it."

Why, I didn't even like to say the word. But I knew if I didn't tell Wisteria, she'd never let me be. Just like if I didn't tell her about Sondra, she wouldn't let me be.

So I told her.

"Me and Kitty were walking up to the pond one really hot summer day. I couldn't have been more than seven years old. I wasn't allowed to go swimming all by myself, but Mama said I could go up to the pond and get my feet wet a little, just as long as I took Kitty along with me. Well, I wasn't watching where I was walking—you know how careless little kids can be—and I stepped right on a copperhead with my bare foot."

"Yikes!" Wisteria screamed and shivered all over.

"Now, I know it was only protecting itself, but that snake reared back to strike at me. I just froze and screamed bloody murder. Kitty saw it all happen and heard me scream, of course, so he jumped between me and that copperhead just in the nick of time, protecting me from being bit. But that copperhead bit Kitty, bit him right in his face. It hurt him bad, too, and he cried real hard. That's why I'm so scared of snakes, 'cause it hurt my dog so bad. And that's also why I love my Kitty so much."

"How'd Kitty get all right?"

"Well, I screamed and screamed so loud Daddy could hear me all the way down to his garden. He came flying up the path and grabbed both me and Kitty up, one of us under each arm, and started running back to the house. I was still screaming and Kitty was crying and yelping. Mama was at the kitchen window, so Daddy yelled to her, 'Brenda, I gotta take Kitty down to Doc Smoot. He's been bit by a copperhead.' Mama yelled, 'Is Bit okay?' Daddy promised her I was and then said, 'Call Doc and tell him I'm on my way.' He put us both in his truck, and we went barreling down the holler road so fast we were bouncing all over the place. Daddy was kicking up so much dust, we could hardly see where we were going. Halfway to town I had quit my screaming and was holding on to Kitty, but he was still whimpering. I just watched as his face got all swolt up, and I couldn't do one single thing at all to help."

"What did Doc Smoot do?" Wisteria asked me.

"Well, he gave him a shot of something to take the swelling down and held him at the dog hospital overnight to keep a watchful eye on him. When we went to get him the next day, his swolt-up face had gone down a bunch and he was real happy to see me."

"Well, that explains everything. I can understand how Katy Perry would be a reminder of that frightful experience, even though she's nothing but a stuffy," she said, standing up on my chair and crawling onto my vanity. Then she stood on the vanity on her tiptoes and reached up behind my other stuffies and pulled Katy Perry down. "So, again, I promise I'll keep her away from you."

"Thanks, Wisteria. I'm counting on it."

She climbed into bed and crawled under the covers, stuffing Katy Perry underneath with her. I turned off the light and crawled in after her.

"Night, Bit."

"Night, Wisteria."

We had worked like the very dickens that day, stocking all the new inventory. And hearing Wisteria be so sad just sucked what little energy I had left right out of me. I was so tired, even my bones hurt a little.

Mama called the bone-hurting part growing pains. I could already feel myself drifting off to sleep before I could get my pillow fluffed up and turned to the cool side. And in my fuzziness I could hear Wisteria humming "Jesus Take the Wheel."

* * *

At seven o'clock the next morning, Daddy whispered, "Wake up, girls. I've fixed y'all some pancakes and bacon. Hurry, now. We gotta get Wisteria home so she can get ready to have her picture taken. And be real quiet so you won't wake up Mama. She doesn't get to sleep in much anymore."

Wisteria stretched and slipped out of bed, her squeaky-clean hair hanging almost to the hem of her pajamas.

I got up and headed to pee, but not before I said, "And, Wisteria, don't you leave here until you put Katy Perry back up on that shelf, behind all the other stuffies."

"Will do," she promised.

When I came out of the bathroom, Wisteria was standing on her tiptoes on my vanity, putting Katy Perry right back where she belonged.

"There you go, Bit. All safe from scary memories. Now I want some of your daddy's pancakes."

So she hopped off the vanity, raced me to the kitchen, and was already sitting at the table in front of one of Daddy's breakfast plates, heaped with his golden pancakes and crunchy bacon.

"This is so yummy, Mr. Harrison," Wisteria said, her mouth full.

"Why, thank you, Wisteria. I'm not much of a cook, but I do make a mean pancake."

"Yes, you do," Wisteria said, licking the syrup off her lips.

"Thanks, Daddy."

When Daddy got up to pour himself another cup of coffee, Wisteria leaned over to me and whispered, "Your daddy is as nice as your mama."

She smiled at me but only with her lips. Her eyes weren't smiling at all.

"Well, I better be getting dressed and heading on home. I gotta get all prissied up like a d...." She caught herself before she cussed in front of Daddy and said, "Like a daggone sissy. And Mama has to French braid my hair." She wiped her mouth on the back of her hand and said, "Thanks, Mr. Harrison, for the breakfast. That was delicious."

"You're most welcome, Wisteria. The next time I'm on pancake duty, I'll let you know."

"I'll be here, Mr. Harrison," Wisteria said, as she slid off her chair and ran to get dressed.

* * *

Later that morning I was practicing my piano lesson, struggling with Mozart's "Sonata Facile in C." Miss Mercy had assigned it to me the past week because she said she wanted to challenge me. Well, I was so challenged that I just gave up and started playing my old stand-by, "Für Elise."

I recognized Wisteria's fast and loud banging on the door. Don't know why she didn't just barge on in. She barged into everything else she did. But she'd bang real hard and fast and then wait for somebody to answer the door and invite her in. So I cut "Für Elise" short, closed up my piano, and went to let her in.

When I opened the door, there stood Wisteria in a fancy yellow dress and black patent-leather shoes. Miss Faylene had tied big yellow bows to the ends of her French braids, and they hung down over her shoulders.

"Oh, Wisteria, you look beautiful!"

"Do not! I look like a damn sissy, and you know it. But the news isn't all bad, Bit," she said, charging on in the house, her stiff new shoes clacking on the hardwood floor.

"What's the not-bad news, Wisteria."

"I'm sure that Daddy Earl has finally seen the error of his ways and is going to stop being up to no good, once and for all."

"That's great, Wisteria. What happened to make you think that?"

"Well, the whole family got all gussied up, as you can plainly see," she said, twirling all the way around so I could plainly see, "and we took off down there to Mr. Simpson's photography studio. Mama looked beautiful in her pale blue Sunday dress and white high heels. She had her long brown hair all pulled back in a pearl barrette, and you could see her big blue eyes so good. And she wore the pearl necklace that Daddy Earl had given her when they got married. I heard Daddy Earl say, 'Faylene, I don't ever remember seeing you look so pretty.' And then he held her hand! Then when Mr. Simpson was arranging us to have our picture took, he set Daddy Earl down on the bench first. Then he had Mama sit right in front of him real close and lean her head up against Daddy Earl's cheek. Then he placed Daddy Earl's hand on Mama's leg. And when Mr. Simpson was trying to get the rest of us situated, I saw Daddy Earl smile and pat Mama on the leg. So, Bit, I just know everything is going to be all right. Isn't that good news?"

"Yeah, Wisteria, that's the best news ever."

"Well, I gotta go now. Mama said she'd have my hide if I did anything to this damn sissy dress. Also, we're having bologna and cheese sandwiches and potato chips for lunch, and Daddy Earl is going to eat bologna and cheese sandwiches and potato chips with us."

Then she twirled her yellow dress toward the door. When she got there, she did a quick little tap dance on the hardwood floor and flew out the door and jumped off the porch.

She ran across the front yard, screaming, "Ain't got time for you today, Kitty. Catch you next time."

Then she streaked on up the holler road, pumping her arms real hard, and disappeared around the bend.

* * *

In about a week Mr. Simpson had the Jones family's picture order ready, and Miss Faylene went downtown to pick it up.

That afternoon Wisteria came pounding on the door, screaming, "Open up, Bit, I got the greatest thing to show you."

When I opened the door, Wisteria, grinning wider than ever, shoved her family's Baptist Church directory picture at me, saying, "Look! Look, isn't it wonderful?"

There in the picture were the seven Joneses, all smiling like the great big happy family Wisteria wished they could be.

"That one's for you," she said. "You can stick it on your vanity mirror. That way you'll always remember me. I got another copy for myself. I keep it right here," she said, patting the overalls pocket over her heart.

"Now, go stick yours on your mirror before it gets all wrinkled up. And I gotta run on home. I want to see Daddy Earl's face when he comes home from work and sees our beautiful family picture that'll be in the Baptist Church directory."

And she jumped off our front porch and flew out the yard and up the holler road. She had chucked her new patent-leather shoes and was back to running like the wind in her magic orange high-tops.

* * *

Wisteria always carries her Baptist Church directory picture in her overalls pocket, and she'll take it out when she needs to remind herself that one time the whole Jones family was really happy and smiling.

FOURTEEN

Celebratin' at
Uncle Double
and Aunt Too's

We were sitting on the dock with our feet dangling in the pond. The lake level had risen from the last big rain, and Wisteria had grown a smidgen since our last trip to the pond, so her toes finally reached the water.

I said, "Uncle Double and Aunt Too are having a Fourth of July party. Want to go with me?"

"Is Purdy Boy going?"

"No, I didn't invite him. I invited you."

Actually, Palmer Lee wasn't going to be in town for the Fourth of July. His mama had to go back home to Raleigh for a couple of days to instruct their gardeners about planting some bushes around their pool. And then the whole family was invited to a pig pickin' over at the governor's mansion. I hadn't ever known a soul who had been invited to the governor's mansion. Course, I'd taken that field trip on the school bus back in fifth grade to visit the governor's mansion. But that was different. We weren't formally invited; we just went. Anyway, Palmer Lee wasn't going to be around for the Fourth of July, but Wisteria didn't need to know that. What she needed to believe was that she was my first choice.

"In that case, sure, I'll go. Just what will we do at Uncle Double and Aunt Too's Fourth of July party?" she asked. "Shoot off firecrackers and stuff?"

"Well, it's really lots of fun. Everybody takes a potluck dish, but you don't have to take anything. Mama will fix enough for all of us. She usually takes potato salad and Jell-O with mandarin oranges and bananas. You know, that's Buddy's favorite. She also bakes a pecan pie and a chocolate meringue pie. So, you see, there's no need for you to bring a thing."

"Okay. I was thinking of maybe asking Mama to cook some squirrel with cream gravy for me to take to the party, but I can see that won't be necessary."

"Nah, Uncle Double will cook hot dogs and hamburgers on the grill, so we won't be needing Miss Faylene's squirrel with cream gravy."

I was so relieved for those hot dogs and hamburgers, because I didn't think squirrel with cream gravy was fitting Fourth of July picnic food.

"Well, we'll play games, like corn hole and horseshoes and softball. Then we'll eat a whole bunch of food. Daddy will even make us a churn of peach ice cream with the local peaches Mama got over the weekend at the Mount Pine Farmer's Market. Uncle Double will cut open a couple of watermelons, and the little kids will have a watermelon-seed-spitting contest. Then when the sun goes down, the daddies will set off fireworks."

"Well, you can just count me in on all that stuff, 'cause that sounds like my kind of fun."

"Good. And Aunt Too will make one of those big sheet cakes all decorated like an American flag."

"You know, I like your Aunt Too a lot, not as much as I love Miss Brenda, of course, but a whole lot. But you haven't ever told me why you call her Aunt Too."

"You mean you didn't uncover that in your research?" I teased.

"Nope, sure didn't."

"Well, that's a pretty amusing story."

"Oh, good, you know how I love an amusing story. I love to tell 'em, love to hear 'em. So tell me. I'm all ears."

"Well, I don't believe that for a minute, Wisteria, but, anyway, you know my Uncle Ted is married to Aunt Sally."

"Yeah, I know your Aunt Sally real good. She has red hair just like me. Well, not to split hairs, ha, my hair is technically orange, but I guess you would say we are both redheads, 'cause you wouldn't say somebody was an orangehead. And, you know, your Aunt Sally was my little sister Faye's second grade school teacher this year. And next year she's gonna be my little sister Virginia's second grade school teacher. She is real nice, and when Mama and Daddy Earl went to PTA on meet-the-teacher night, your Aunt Sally said how smart Faye is and what a delight she is to teach and how she is pleased to know that she is going to have another Jones child in her class next year. But what does your Aunt Sally have to do with why you call your other aunt Too?"

"Well, Wisteria, I was getting to that before you took my entertaining story into a whole 'nother direction."

"Oh, okay, then, I'm all ears."

"I still don't believe that, Wisteria," I said, "but, anyway, Uncle Ted is married to Aunt Sally, and Uncle Double is married to a Sally too."

"Oh, I get it! She's a Sally too. How neat is that?"

"Well, there's even more to the story. So, Wisteria, I know you'll be all ears."

"You got it," she said and pretended to zip her lips and lock them.

"So Mama says to Buddy, who's just two years old at the time, 'Uncle Ted married a lady named Sally, and now Uncle Double is going to marry a lady named Sally too.' Buddy stuck up two fingers and said, 'I two too!' Course, everybody laughed, 'cause Buddy was so cute, and then he started calling our aunt Two Too. Soon it just got shortened to Too, like all our long names seem to."

"Like her nickname got a nickname."

"Right."

"Very interesting, but, come to think of it, I don't believe you ever told me how your uncle came to be called Double. Now, don't quote me on this, but that's a right unusual name for a gentleman like your uncle."

I laughed at Wisteria and told her, "Yes, it's quite unusual, but there's a story behind his name too. I mean *also*."

"Good one, Bit," Wisteria said and winked at me. "Now, give it to me."

"Well, Uncle Double's given name is Trailor, which is a family name. When he was a teenager, his friends said it sounded just like *trailer*—you know, one of those houses on wheels."

"Sure, Bit, I know what a trailer is. Remember I lived in one down by the river for a good while."

"Oh, yeah, that's right. Well, anyway, since his name sounded like *trailer*, his friends started calling him Double Wide. Somewhere along the way, they shortened it to Double, and it just stuck."

"Well, Bit, I gotta tell you, I didn't think it could get any more interesting that the story about your Aunt Too's name, but I believe you just topped yourself. I hope you don't mind if I quote you. I'd love to pass those amusing tidbits on to just about everybody I know. I think they would be good supper conversations, don't you?"

"Sure, Wisteria, they're all yours."

"Well, I want to get all my facts straight," she said, as she started mumbling to herself.

* * *

"Has anybody heard from Ted?"

We'd been at Uncle Double and Aunt Too's Fourth of July party for about an hour and a half. Uncle Ted was planning to close up the drugstore around four and head on up with some ice and salt for the ice cream churn. Daddy was beginning to get worried. If Uncle Ted was going to be late, he usually called.

Aunt Sally said, "Oh, Harrison, don't you worry. He'll be here before too long."

Just as soon as Aunt Sally said that, Uncle Ted came pulling up in the yard. He got out of his car and started toward us with his hands in his pockets and his eyes on the ground. We noticed he still had on his work clothes—hadn't even gone home to take off his pharmacist's smock and put on his jeans. And he wasn't toting any ice and salt either.

"What's a matter, Ted?" Uncle Double said, when he saw his brother coming toward him, dressed like a pharmacist.

"Maudie Puckett came in the store this afternoon, just when I was getting ready to close up. She was crying and wailing so hard I couldn't figure out what in the world was wrong with her. When I finally got some Co-Cola in her and got her settled down, she told me she went out to feed her chickens and found that two of her prize Rhode Island Reds were missing."

"Missing?" asked my daddy. "You suppose a fox got 'em? Please don't tell me we've got another mountain lion in the holler. Won't anything be safe if that's the case."

"No, Harrison," Uncle Ted said, "Sheriff Roudebush went up to Maudie's with me. Said it didn't look like a fox or a mountain lion, 'cause there's no sign of blood or feathers. They've simply vanished, just like all the other animals."

"Still no idea what's happening to them?"

"No idea, Harrison. It's just baffling."

Well, that put a terrible damper on the party. After that, there wasn't any mention of seed-spitting contests or fireworks. All anybody wanted to talk about was the disappearance of the Lovington pets. The adults finally gave up, cut the party short, and everybody just went on home.

* * *

First time a Lovington pet disappeared, folks just found it odd. After the second, third, and so forth time, people got mad and confused.

"Ain't nothing safe no more," said Miss Tallulah Prevatte. "I guess we're just gonna have to start locking our doors. I know Daddy, God rest his soul, is spinning in his grave over all this mayhem."

"Why, I ain't been this upset since they sent my Junior over yonder to Afghanistan," Miz Nola Reavis said, honking her nose into her hanky and dabbing at her puffy, red eyes.

"Calm down, ladies," said Sheriff Roudebush. "You're blowing this thing out of proportion. I don't believe we need to be living in fear or comparing what's happening to a war. Ain't no people missing—yet. So, please settle down. You're scarin' the young'uns."

The ladies had congregated in The Quilt Shop, and Mama and Miss Nelda were just beside themselves with worry. Crazy, wailing ladies weren't good for business. But wail they would, so Mama had called Sheriff Roudebush to come over and try to calm them down. But nothing seemed to be working. They were hysterical, and no matter what anybody said, they just got shriller and shriller over whoever was swiping the town's pets.

While the ladies were crying and blowing their noses on their lace hankies and trying to convince Sheriff Roudebush that we were all in grave danger, in strolled Palmer Lee, all fresh and smiling from his weekend at the club and the governor's mansion over at the Capital.

"What's going on?" he asked, when he got to the back of the store. "Why are those ladies crying like that?"

Wisteria was on a ladder, stocking top shelves, and she acted like Palmer Lee wasn't even there. She'd have loved to be the one to tell about the most recent disappearance, but Palmer Lee just wasn't worth her energy. So she didn't even bother speaking to him.

"Well," I said, "you missed a bunch of excitement while you were over to the Capital."

"More excitement in Lovington? You're kidding."

"Somebody took off with Miss Maudie Puckett's prize Rhode Island Red chickens. And, remember, we haven't even gotten over Lord Poodle and Chirp and Larue's disappearances yet."

"Yeah, Larue, the goose that sings the national anthem, right?"

"Same one," I said. "So those ladies are real upset about it."

"Why would somebody take the lady's chickens? Were they planning to eat them?"

I heard Wisteria let out a "Pfft!"

I turned toward her just in time to see her roll her eyes at Palmer Lee. She found his city-slicker ways rather naïve for country living.

"Nobody knows why anyone would take prize Rhode Island Red chickens," I said. "And I'm guessing they didn't take 'em to eat, 'cause whoever did it probably took Lord Poodle too. And I'm guessing nobody wants to eat a dog."

"But, once again, my name has been cleared," Wisteria said, wanting it known, even to Palmer Lee, that she'd never steal a beloved pet.

"I'm sure it has, Wisteria. I can't imagine you taking someone's chickens."

Wisteria just rolled her eyes again.

"The reason I came by was to see if you wanted to go to lunch," Palmer Lee said. "I thought maybe we could go over to your Uncle Ted's for a grilled cheese sandwich."

"I brought my lunch today, Palmer Lee," I said and looked up to see Wisteria squinching up her eyes at me.

"Can you save it till tomorrow?" Palmer Lee asked.

I thought about it for a minute and ignored Wisteria's squinched-up eyes and said, "Sure, I'd like that."

"Great," he said, "I'll stop back by at noon. How's that?"

"Fine. That'll work just great."

He kissed me on the cheek and turned to leave. My insides went all skittery as I watched him walk to the front of the shop and out the door. I went on back to work.

Wisteria wouldn't talk to me. She didn't talk to me for the rest of the morning.

When Palmer Lee came back to fetch me at noon, Wisteria and I were stocking shelves in silence, trying to find a spot for Miss Enid Ransom's tea towels with cross stitch bunnies and flowers on them and white eyelet lace all around the edges. Those towels were proof that tourists would buy anything.

I heard the bell tinkle when the front door opened and saw Palmer Lee stroll in, his hands in the pockets, his blonde hair hanging over to one side.

"Hey, Mrs. Sizemore," I heard him say.

"Hi, Palmer Lee," Mama called out.

"Is Bit ready for lunch?" he asked Mama.

"I believe so. She and Wisteria are over there, stocking shelves."

He smiled when he saw me and made my heart flutter. He looked so handsome in his polo shirt, this one robin-egg blue that matched his eyes perfectly, and he wore his deck shoes without socks, showing off his tan legs covered with golden hair.

"Purdy Boy," Wisteria spat under her breath, but just loud enough for me to hear.

"Stop it, Wisteria!"

"Just be careful is all I'm sayin'," she said, flinging tea towels real mad-like.

"Hey," Palmer Lee said when he got close enough to lean in and secret-squeeze my hand. "You hungry?"

He smelled real clean, like Dial soap and Crest toothpaste.

"Sure. Wisteria, I'll be back in a little while. You want me to bring you a grilled cheese from Uncle Ted's?"

"Nope, brought my lunch with me, like I always do," she said, without even looking my way.

"Okay, bye," was all there was left for me to say.

"Mama, we're going down to Uncle Ted's for a grilled cheese. Y'all want something?"

Both Mama and Miss Nelda said, "No, thanks," and then Mama added, "hurry back. We need your help. The place is filling up."

Sure enough, folks were buzzing all around, and a tour bus had just pulled up in front of the store, full of ladies wanting quilts and primitive art and tea towels and bird houses.

"Yes, ma'am, we won't be long."

Once we were out of sight of The Quilt Shop, Palmer Lee took my hand and laced his fingers through mine, making my heart do that fluttery thing again.

When we got to Uncle Ted's drugstore, Palmer Lee opened the door and held it for me real polite and gentlemanly.

Uncle Ted was up behind his pharmacy counter, and I yelled out, "Hey, Uncle Ted!"

"Hey, Bit, Palmer Lee. You not working today, Bit?"

"Yes, sir, I am, but me and Palmer Lee just came over to get us a sandwich."

We sat down at the counter and Selma asked, "What y'all want?"

Selma had a pencil behind her ear in case she had a real long order that she couldn't remember. I'd never seen her get an order so long she couldn't remember it, though, and that pencil stayed behind her ear from the time she came to work in the morning until she walked out the door every evening.

"I'll take a grilled cheese and a Cherry Co-Cola, Selma," I said.

Palmer Lee said, "And I'll have the same, Miss Selma." And to me he said, "Let's get a Cherry Coke for Wisteria too."

I smiled at his thoughtfulness but said, "Nah, she didn't even drink the last one we took her."

Selma fixed our lunch, and Uncle Ted called across the drugstore, "On the house, Selma."

"Course it is, Ted," she called back.

"Thanks, y'all," I told Selma and Uncle Ted and bit into my sandwich.

Selma makes the best grilled cheese sandwiches on the face of the earth. They're grilled real crunchy and buttery on the outside, and the cheese is real gooey and stringy on the inside. After she grills them, she opens them up and puts lettuce and tomatoes on them. Selma's grilled cheese is one of my all-time favorite foods, next to my mama's fried chicken. And goin'-to-school cookies, of course.

When we'd finished our lunch, I said, "I gotta run. Mama needs me real bad at the shop."

"Sure," Palmer Lee said, "I understand."

So after Palmer Lee put some money on the counter for Selma's tip, we said, "Bye," and headed on back to The Quilt Shop. When we got there, we saw Wisteria sitting on the bench in front of the shop, eating her peanut butter sandwich and banging her orange high-tops together.

FIFTEEN

Wisteria Sets Out
to Prove She's
Better 'n Purdy Boy

"Hey, Wisteria," we both said when we got close. Without even looking at us, she pointed to her mouth to show us she couldn't talk with her mouth full of peanut butter sandwich. Talking with her mouth full never seemed to bother her before. We just ignored her.

"Well, I'd better run," Palmer Lee said. "Daddy wants me to come up to the lodge this afternoon."

When Wisteria heard Palmer Lee say that, she swallowed real quick, swiped her hand across her mouth, and asked, "Just what are you doing up here in the sticks anyway, Palmer Lee Compton?"

Not taking Wisteria's bait or even getting mad at how rude Wisteria was to him, he just said to her, "Well, I'm helping Daddy oversee the building of his hunting lodge. He wants it done before fall, and he thinks we have to stay right on top of things if we want it finished on schedule."

"Hunting lodge, huh? Do you even know how to shoot a gun, Purdy Boy?"

"Yes, I do, Wisteria. I'm on the rifle team at school."

"Oh, are you now?" she said, real sassy-like. "And what do you do on that rifle team? March all over the football field at half-time, tossing and twirling a toy gun?"

"That's a precision team, Wisteria, not a rifle team. We actually have a shooting range on campus. I practice every afternoon during the school year."

"Well, hmmpf," Wisteria said. "Bet you can't hit a moving squirrel right 'tween the eyes, now can you?"

"Never tried, Wisteria."

"Well, hang around, Purdy Boy, and I'll show you how it's done. Then I'll demonstrate how you skin that sucker with one hand."

Feeling that she had put that city boy in his place, she returned her attention to her peanut butter sandwich until Palmer Lee said, "I don't believe in killing innocent animals."

"Well, what's the sense in learning to shoot a damn gun if you're not going to go hunting for animals?" Wisteria snapped at him.

I said, "Shush, Wisteria. Mama's customers are going to hear you cussing, and Mama isn't going to like that, one little bit."

Wisteria squinted her eyes at me and kept on mouthing off to Palmer Lee.

"Bet you don't mind eating animals that someone else killed, though, do you? You know, that steak you eat up there at that highfalutin club of yours came off a live cow!" Wisteria snapped.

Still Palmer Lee refused to get angry at Wisteria. Instead, he just said, "Yes, Wisteria, I know that steak comes from a cow. But I don't eat steak. And I don't eat chicken or pork. I'm a vegetarian, because I don't believe in killing and eating animals. I love animals. I just enjoy shooting at targets. It's a sport."

"Sport, pffft!" Wisteria spat.

Palmer Lee ignored Wisteria's scorn and said, "I'd like to practice during summer break, but I haven't had a chance since I've been up here. I can't seem to find a range."

"Can't find a range, huh? Well, what if I find you a range?" Wisteria said.

"That would be great. Do you know where one is?"

"Damn straight, I do. Tell you what, I'll find you a range, and then I'll challenge you to a shooting match."

"Sounds good, Wisteria, but rumor has it you're a pretty good shot."

"I'm more 'n good, Purdy Boy. I'm *damn* good!"

I just shook my head, but Palmer Lee laughed at her and said, "You name the time and place and your choice of weapons. I'll be there."

Without even hesitating, like she'd been thinking about this for a long time, she said, "Twenty-twos, noon, Saturday. Bit'll give you directions to the range."

And Wisteria went on back to eating her lunch, looking all smug, like she'd already won that match and showed Palmer Lee who was the rifle-shooting boss around Lovington.

* * *

Now, we really don't have a shooting range, so to speak, in Lovington. It's just a piece of old worn-out fence up the holler in a clearing above Mose Beemus's former property, which just happened to belong to Senator Fletcher Compton now, since he cut that deal with Mose.

All week Wisteria scoured town for targets: plastic bottles, soda bottles, tin cans. She plundered through garbage cans, recycle bins, and dumpsters. She collected everything she could find that she could use to prove to Palmer Lee Compton that she was better than he was, at least at one thing. Buddy agreed to fill the bed of his truck with Wisteria's junk and drive it up to the shooting range for her, so she could get ready for her challenge with Purdy Boy.

Saturday around eleven o'clock Palmer Lee showed up at my house wearing blue jeans, a white tee shirt, and tennis shoes. I didn't even know he owned such clothes, but I was glad he hadn't worn monogrammed khaki Bermudas and a pink plaid shirt. Just not appropriate attire for a holler shooting match.

He had his twenty-two under his arm, and he said, "Ready to go?"

"Sure," I said and called to Mama that we were leaving.

Mama came out of the kitchen, a spatula in her hand. "Hey, Palmer Lee. Now, you children be very careful, you hear? And, Bit, you stay with Buddy while the shooting is going on. You know the safety rules."

"Yes, ma'am."

Then Palmer Lee told her, "We'll be careful, Mrs. Sizemore."

Palmer Lee didn't hold my hand, like usual, while we were walking up the holler road. Instead, he concentrated on holding on to his twenty-two real careful. When we got up to Wisteria's shooting range, we saw that Luke and Buddy were already there—along with about every other guy from Lovington. Apparently, boys love a challenge, and they wouldn't miss one for the world. Girls, not so much. I was the only girl there, except for Wisteria, of course.

Wisteria had already lined up ten targets along the fence, and when she saw us come up, she said, "Hey, Bit. Hey, Purdy Boy. Now, here's the rules. As you can see, I have already set up the first round of targets. There will be ten targets per round. You get ten shots per round. Buddy here will reset the targets after each round.

We'll shoot ten rounds each. My brother Luke here is going to keep score for us. You agree to that, Purdy Boy?"

Palmer Lee had gotten so used to Wisteria calling him Pretty Boy, that he didn't even object, just told her, "Sure, Wisteria, I trust Luke to be a fair score keeper."

Then Palmer Lee nodded over at Luke and reached out to shake his hand in agreement.

"Buddy here's gonna toss a coin to see who'll go first. Fine by you?"

"Fine by me," said Palmer Lee.

Wisteria called, "Heads," and Buddy flipped the coin high in the air. When it came back down, it landed square in the palm of his left hand, and he slapped it good with his right. When he lifted his right hand to peek, he said, "Heads it is."

Wisteria had won the toss.

She grinned real smug-like at Palmer Lee and said, "You're on."

First round out Wisteria stepped up to her spot, raised her twenty-two to her shoulder, took a real deep breath, peered down the barrel, and proceeded to hit all ten of her targets, sending each one sailing till the fence rail was bare.

When she was sure she'd cleared her first round, she lowered her gun, looked real confident at Palmer Lee, and said, "Match that, Purdy Boy."

"Great job," Palmer Lee said, as Wisteria stepped aside and he took her place.

Palmer Lee looked real sure of himself when he lifted his gun to his shoulder. He fired real quick and hit the first seven targets. Then he missed number eight. Without saying a word, he took out numbers nine and ten real easy.

"Hmmm, not bad for a big-city purdy boy. I may have misjudged you," Wisteria said, as she stepped back up to take on round number two.

Just like her first round, her second round was perfect. So was Palmer Lee's.

When he finished his round, Wisteria said, "Damn," under her breath.

Luke said, "Wisteria, cut out that cussing."

Without looking Luke's way, she mumbled, "Ain't cussin', just quotin'."

Both of them hit ten out of ten targets for the next three rounds, and each time Palmer Lee finished a round, all Wisteria would say was, "Damn."

But she'd stopped telling him he wasn't bad for a big-city purdy boy.

Then on round six Wisteria made her first mistake. After hitting six targets off the fence, she grazed number seven just slightly, spun it around, tipped it over, but left it laying on the fence.

"But you hit it, Wisteria, even knocked it over," Palmer Lee said.

"Doesn't matter. I didn't knock it off the fence, so it's a miss."

"If you say so, Wisteria," Palmer Lee said, and changed places with her again.

Palmer Lee's sixth round was perfect. He and Wisteria were even.

This time she really said, "Damn!"

Luke had stopped telling her to cut out the cussing.

They both hit all ten targets on round seven. They were still tied.

Round eight, once again, Wisteria hit all her targets.

Then Palmer Lee started his eighth round by missing the very first target. Taking a deep breath, he took out numbers two through eight. Then he missed nine but hit ten.

He was two points behind Wisteria.

Going into round nine Wisteria was starting to feel like she had this one in the bag. She was really going to show Purdy Boy who was best. And who was boss.

She was knocking her round nine targets off *ping! ping! ping!* until she got to number ten...and missed.

Then Palmer Lee had a perfect round nine.

Going into the last round, Wisteria was still quotin', and she was only one point ahead of Palmer Lee. Then, during that very last round, her nerves seemed to get the best of her. Sweat broke out on her lip, and she started to miss. She'd been hitting nine or ten targets each time, but this time she was missing every other shot. Halfway through, she lowered her rifle, let out a big whoosh of air, raked her arm across her forehead, and wiped her damp hands on the legs of her overalls. Then she put her twenty-two to her shoulder and commenced to finish her round. In the end she'd hit only five targets. That meant going into his final round, Palmer Lee had to hit just seven of his targets to beat Wisteria.

I knew that he could do it with one hand tied behind his back.

Wisteria knew it too.

She looked like somebody had let the air right out of her.

My heart hurt so bad for her, and tears started stinging my eyes. Palmer Lee had everything, including some of her best friend's time. And, as far as we knew, he didn't have a daddy who was up to no good. Wisteria deserved to beat Palmer Lee at the one thing she did best—shooting a gun.

When Palmer Lee stepped up to his mark for his last round, I started saying in my head, *Miss it, miss it, miss it.*

He missed number one but hit numbers two, three, and four easy.

"Damn!" Wisteria said.

Just four more to win.

Then Palmer Lee missed number five but hit number six.

Then Wisteria said, "Damn!" again.

Then he hit number seven. But Palmer Lee's nerves must have been getting to him, too, 'cause he missed number eight.

He had only two more targets, and he needed to hit them both to beat Wisteria.

And then he missed nine.

Only one point behind Wisteria, and he had just one Clorox bottle to go. It was big. He couldn't miss it.

"Nail this one, Purdy Boy, and we go to sudden death," Wisteria said under her breath.

Without looking her way or saying a word, Palmer Lee put that twenty-two to his shoulder, looked down that barrel, and pulled the trigger.

And missed.

That crowd of guys, who had been so quiet the whole time, with their legs all splayed wide and their arms crossed over their chests, started screaming and jumping around and punching each other on the shoulder and patting Wisteria on the back.

And I was so happy for her.

She squeezed her way out of that crowd of screaming guys and walked over to Palmer Lee. She stuck out her hand and said, "Great match, Palmer Lee. I'm impressed."

Then she tucked her twenty-two under her arm, turned, and sauntered down the holler road toward her respectable three-bed-room, one-and-one-half bath, brick ranch-style house.

SIXTEEN

Daddy Earl Must be Fishing 'Cause He Always Brings Home a Big Old Mess of Trout

That following weekend Palmer Lee was gone, back home to Raleigh he said. I expected Wisteria to be happy as could be because she had beaten Palmer Lee fair and square, and the two of us were gonna spend all day Saturday together. Alone.

We'd packed peanut butter and banana sandwiches, a can of Pringles, and Mama's homemade dill pickles and had toted our lunch up to the pond. We sat down at the end of the dock, and Wisteria reached into our sack and began doling out sandwiches and all the rest.

Wisteria had just taken a bite of her sandwich when she opened her mouth to say something. That bite got stuck to the roof of her mouth, and she said, "Mwufl dwath."

We both laughed so hard that Wisteria's lunch flew out of her mouth, into the pond. Then that tickled me so much that I laughed till I wasn't making any sound at all. I was laying back on the dock, holding my stomach while the tears streamed out of my eyes and into my ears. It took me a real long while before I could sit back up and dry off my face and ears with the bottom of my tee shirt. When I did, Wisteria wasn't laughing any more.

"That was real funny, Bit, but what I was aiming to say isn't funny a'tall."

So I tried to get serious, which is real hard when you've been laughing like crazy. "What'sa matter, Wisteria?"

Concentrating hard on her scabby knee instead of looking me in the eye, she said, "Well, you know Daddy Earl and his buddies go down to Papa Luke's little old rickety trailer by the river on the weekends. They fish for trout, and then they fix Dinty Moore beef stew on that little old two-burner stove in the kitchenette in the trailer. Leastwise, that's what Daddy Earl says he's doing. Mama doesn't believe him. She says he's still up to no good down there."

I understood that Wisteria didn't have anybody else to tell this stuff to, but I was still uncomfortable hearing her talk about it—especially after she'd already told me that Mr. Earl had mended his ways after the Jones family got their picture taken for the Baptist Church directory. But I was Wisteria's best friend, and best friends sometimes gotta take a little discomfort for each other. So I just kept my eyes on the pond and my words to myself and let her do all the talking.

"But I can't believe it's true, Bit. Daddy Earl sings in the Baptist choir, and I don't think they'd let a person sing in the Baptist choir if he was up to no good. Do you think?"

I said, "Probably not," but I had no idea how the Baptist choir worked. Maybe before they handed you your choir robe, they made you sign a pledge that said you wouldn't be up to no good as long as you were a member of the Baptist choir.

"And something else, Bit, how can Daddy Earl be up to no good when he's spending all his away time fishing? And I know he's fishing 'cause he always comes home with a big old mess of trout."

When Wisteria said that about believing her daddy was fishing because he always brought home a mess of trout, my heart hurt so bad, like somebody had grabbed it and punched it real hard. And this is why.

It was late one Saturday afternoon Mama said to me, "Bit, go down to the Piggly Wiggly and pick me up some Crisco, will you? I seem to be running short, and I plan to bake a pecan pie for tomorrow's bake sale at the church." She gave me some money and said, "And get yourself a Baby Ruth."

I went out to the shed to get my bike. When I pulled it out in the yard, Kitty woke up and acted like he was gonna follow me.

I said, "Go on back to sleep. You can't go with me this time."

So he flopped back down and went on back to snoozing.

I told Buddy, "He's really a smart dog. He understands what I say."

Buddy says, "Nah, he doesn't. He wouldn't've followed you anyway. He was just curious and wanted to know what you were up to. He was planning on laying down and going on back to sleep all along. He's too lazy to walk to town."

Still thinking my dog was real smart, I took off down the holler road on my bike and hung a right when I reached Main Street, headed for the Piggly Wiggly, right next to the post office. I remembered telling Miss O.O. that we'd come visit her at the post office soon, back when me and Wisteria were handing out our fliers, looking for work. And since I hadn't lived up to that promise, I made a mental note to drop in the next time I was in town and not in a hurry to get Crisco for my mama. I pulled into the bike stand next to the front doors and went on inside the Piggly Wiggly. That's when I saw Wisteria's Daddy Earl at the check-out.

"Hey, Mr. Earl," I said.

"How ya doin', Miss Bit. Where's your sidekick?"

"We've been swimming up at the pond all afternoon. She went on home to help Miss Faylene with supper."

Then Charmaine DuPriest, the Piggly Wiggly cashier, popped her gum real loud and said, "That'll be nine-ninety-four, Earl honey."

Then she picked up a big old plastic bag full of trout off the conveyor belt and dropped it in a grocery sack.

After he paid Charmaine, Mr. Earl said, "Well, Bit, I'll see you later."

"Sure thing, Mr. Earl. Tell Miss Faylene I said hey!"

"I'll do that. Bye now, Bit."

Then I watched him head for the Piggly Wiggly door, his sack of trout swinging back and forth from his hand.

I really didn't think anything of it then—didn't have any reason to till Wisteria said that thing about her Daddy Earl fishing and bringing home a mess of trout.

Then it brought to mind something else that happened that involved talk of Mr. Earl.

One morning Wisteria and I walked into The Quilt Shop, and Mama said, "Good lord, Bit, what happened to your hair? Looks like you combed it with the blender this morning."

Wisteria and Miss Nelda laughed, but it embarrassed me to no end. It really was a mess. I must've slept on it all caddywampus, and it was sticking out every which-a-way. Also it was humid that day, and my hair was curlier than ever. I'd tried to tamp it down with some water, but I hadn't had much luck.

"I'm gonna give Shelby Jean a call and see if she can fit you in for a trim this morning."

"Okay, Mama," I said, still embarrassed, and headed on to the storeroom to hide my hair that looked like it had been combed with the blender.

I was standing on a ladder, pulling stuff down to tag and put out for sale, when Mama yelled from the front, "Bit, Shelby Jean says she can fit you in if you come on down right now. Now, scoot and get that hair under control."

I called, "Yes, ma'am," and Wisteria took my place on the ladder.

"I'll be back soon as I can," I told Wisteria, and she said, "I'll hold your place for you."

Mama pulled a wad of bills out of her pocket and handed it to me as I took off running out The Quilt Shop, headed for Miss Shelby Jean's. Shelby Jean Upchurch owns the only beauty parlor in Lovington, and all the ladies in town and some of the men go there to get their hair cut and curled and dyed and whatnot.

When I ran past Uncle Ted's, he stuck his head out the door and called, "Somebody after you, Bit?"

I turned around and started running backwards and yelled, "No, sir, but if I don't get to Miss Shelby Jean's soon to get this hair cut, Mama will be."

Uncle Ted laughed and waved, and I turned around and took off front-ways toward Miss Shelby Jean's.

When I passed Miss Dixie's shop, she was just opening for the morning.

"Hey, sugar," she called.

Miss Dixie calls everybody sugar.

I rounded the corner at Willow Street and dang near tripped over Bug Jeter. He was sitting on the sidewalk, his legs all splayed out, and he was leaning up against the side of Miss Dixie's shop. He was drinking something out of a crumpled brown paper sack. Don't think his Baptist conversion took too good.

By the time I reached Miss Shelby Jean's shop, I was panting and had a hitch in my side, so I had to stand in the doorway for a while, all bent over and breathing real hard.

"You okay, sweetie pie?"

"Yes, ma'am, Miss Shelby Jean. Ran all the way. Got a hitch."

"Well, hop on up here and catch your breath, and we'll wrestle that hair to the ground."

I climbed up in her chair, and she shook out a big pink cape with black poodles all over it and draped it over me.

"The usual?" Miss Shelby Jean asked.

"Yes, ma'am. It's just gotten way too long and sticky-outy."

When she took to cutting, I could hear the other hairdressers, Gaylynn Boney and Velma Nell Upchurch, Shelby Jean's sister-in-law, laughing and talking real loud over at their stations. Then I heard one of them mention Mr. Earl.

"Lord, that's one fine looking man. I'd like me a piece of that. Whoo-ee."

"You got that right, honey. That's one pretty guy, if you ask me. You seen that six pack of his?"

"Whew," said Velma Nell, fanning her face with her hand, "I git all tongue-tied ever' time I lay eyes on that man. Why, look at me. I'm blushing right now just thinking about him."

First off, I didn't see what they were seeing. Sure, Mr. Earl had nice, dark hair and pale, blue eyes just like Wisteria, but he wasn't handsome, like, say, Palmer Lee. He was old, daddy-old, like maybe thirty-eight or forty years old. How could he be daddy-old and still be all the things those ladies were saying?

But they kept on laughing at one another, and Gaylynn said, "That Earl Jones could put his slippers under my bed any time he wanted."

And that's when they laughed the loudest, and Velma Nell reached over and slapped Gaylynn on the shoulder real playful-like and said, "Oh, Gaylynn, shut your mouth. You're just awful!"

I was sitting right there, and those ladies could see me plain as day, but they were talking like maybe my hearing wasn't fully developed yet or something.

Then Rhonda Gail Suthers, who was getting her mousy old brown hair bleached out white, said, "Why, when Earl Jones was captain of the football team down at Lovington High, he could've had any girl he wanted. All's he'd had to do was snap his fingers, and he'd've had any one of us. But what does he do? He goes over there to Cedar Flats, of all places, and hooks up with that tacky, white-trash Faylene Brackett. Course, he wouldn't've married her if he hadn't had to!"

Well, when that bleached-haired Rhonda Gail Suthers said that, Shelby Jean cleared her throat real loud. Everybody shut their yaps and looked over at her. That's when I saw Shelby Jean in the mirror shake her head and cut her eyes at me.

People always say you go to Ted's for news and to Shelby Jean's for scandal. And it hurt me so bad that those ladies were talking scandal about Wisteria's Daddy Earl.

A fish jumped out of the pond right in front of the dock and made a big splash and snapped me out of my day-dreaming.

I noticed that Wisteria was still concentrating on her knee, so I looked out over the pond, because I couldn't look her in the eye, and I said, "I'm pretty sure they won't let anybody sing in the Baptist choir if he's up to no good. And, 'course, Mr. Earl must be down to the river fishing with this buddies if he always comes home with a mess of trout. So, as I see it, Wisteria, you got nothing at all to worry about."

"Yeah," she said, letting her breath out real relieved-like and losing interest in her scab. "That's what I was thinking. It just can't be true. Not my Daddy Earl."

I was bone weary from all the talk about Wisteria's Daddy Earl, and my head was starting to hurt from trying to help her sort everything out in her brain, so I said, "I guess I better be getting on home. Mama's getting pretty fed up with me and Buddy's messy bathroom. I promised her I'd clean it up this afternoon."

"Okay, I better be getting on home too."

Then I watched her get up and drag herself on down the dock. I could tell by the way she was walking that her orange high-tops weren't working their magic and that she wasn't too sure she'd sorted out things about her Daddy Earl just right in her brain.

SEVENTEEN

If Lovington's Good Enough for Senator Compton, Then It's Good Enough for Yella-headed Ladies in Sensible Shoes

When I got home from the pond, Mama was puttering around in the kitchen, baking goin'-to-school cookies and getting our supper ready.

"Go get to work on that bathroom, please. Then you can come help me with supper. Daddy and Buddy are gonna have a long day, what with all the new construction going on, and they're going to be hungry and bone-weary when they get home."

Soon as Senator Compton set to building his lodge up the holler, all those yella-headed ladies started screeching, "Me too! Me too!"

Those rich ladies figured if Lovington was a good enough place for Senator Compton to have a vacation home, then it sure was good enough for them.

So they all went back to wherever they came from and said to their husbands, "I want me a vacation home in Lovington, just like Fletcher Compton."

At least, that's what Daddy figured they'd said.

All we know for sure is, before long those ladies dragged their husbands away from their offices and brought them up to Lovington, looking for a suitable place to build them a home just for playing purposes.

Fitch Howell, who lived down by the river in his family's old run-down homeplace, saw a huge business opportunity in those rich newcomers.

"Them folks don't want to live up a holler. Why, waterfront property is all the rage these days," he said. "They're gonna want to live on the river. And I have just the river-front property for 'em. And, what's more, they'll still have that stunnin' mountain view they're all lookin' for."

So Fitch split up his family's land down by the river into lots just big enough for a nice-size vacation home and advertised his waterfront property with mountain views in the newspaper over in Raleigh and down in Charlotte and even as far away as Roanoke and Richmond, up in Virginia. Daddy said those lots flew off the shelves, and in no time there were plans to build a dozen new houses down by the river, plus a new one for Fitch, soon as he could knock down that old dilapidated heap of a homeplace.

Course, Enoch Murtry over by the bypass and every builder over in Mount Pine had contracts coming out their ears, and they all had to put on new workers. Daddy and Uncle Double got signed on to do the electrical and plumbing for more than half of those houses, and they had to go over to Trident Community College looking for some new electrical and plumbing graduates to help them out.

All the extra work made Daddy so worn out, and he was coming home later and later every night. He was even having to work most Saturdays, which was why he was gonna be tired and late for supper.

"I'm sorry, Bren," he told my mama, "but it won't last long. There's just so much waterfront property to be had in Lovington. And once this is all over, we'll get back to normal, and you can have that new Subaru you have your eye on."

So Mama fixed supper later every night and studied the Subaru brochures she'd picked up over at Weldon Brothers Subaru in Mount Pine to make sure she'd have the exact color and model she wanted when the time came to put in her order.

At first Mr. Hammitt, down at the hardware store, wasn't real certain he liked the competition from the big new Home Depot over by the bypass, but he was pretty darn happy with it now. There wasn't any way he could have kept up with all the contractors' orders for the new vacation houses down by the river.

And even if Mr. Carl loved having to spread his restaurant business out onto the sidewalk, he was glad for the new McDonald's and Taco Bell next to the Home Depot to feed all those construction workers.

And when the new BP station joined the other businesses over by the bypass, Mr. Fisher said, "Thank the lord. I thought I was gonna have to put in some new tanks. My delivery guy said he could go out of his way to service me just so many times each week."

Sure enough, Daddy and Buddy came dragging in, all sweaty and dusty and tired from working all day down by the river, wiring the vacation houses for the yella-headed ladies.

After Daddy and Buddy had washed up and we'd sat down to eat, Daddy said, "Y'all aren't going to believe the transformation down by the river. It doesn't even look like the same place. Course, the houses aren't complete, but you can get a good idea about what it'll be like when we're through."

"Can I go look, Daddy? I want to see all the new houses. Please, please."

Daddy looked kinda like he didn't think that was a great idea till Buddy said, "I'll take her down tomorrow afternoon, if that's okay."

"Well, okay, Buddy, as long as Bit's careful where she steps and doesn't touch anything."

"I'll be careful, Daddy, I promise," I told him.

Then Buddy said, "Bit, let's call Luke and Wisteria and see if they want to go along."

"But Wisteria's not allowed to be my Sunday friend, 'cause we're Piscopalians."

Buddy laughed and said, "Well, just tell Wisteria we promise we won't be drinking wine, and maybe Miss Faylene will say it's okay."

Sure enough, with the promise that we wouldn't be drinking wine on a Sunday afternoon, Miss Faylene said it would be okay if Luke and Wisteria went along with Buddy and me to see the not-yet-finished houses down by the river.

So the next afternoon after church and Sunday dinner, Wisteria and Luke showed up at the house, and the four of us piled into Buddy's truck to go take a look at the transformation down by the river.

Well, boy howdy, we couldn't believe our eyes. It didn't even look like the same place we'd been seeing all our lives. The rocky river bank that used to be all overgrown with big old straggly bushes and brambles that made it so you couldn't even see the river was all cleared out and leveled off and made into nice riverfront lots for houses.

Wisteria screamed, "Sweet baby Jesus on a June bug!" when she laid eyes on it.

Then we started running around, peeking into the windows of the close-to-finished houses.

Buddy was yelling after us, "Now, remember, Daddy said don't touch a thing. And y'all be real careful where you step. A nail could run right through one of those magic orange high-tops of yours, Cuteness."

145

I yelled back, "We'll be careful, Buddy," while I ran after Wisteria and she screamed, "Look at the size of that *kitchen*! It's as big as our whole house."

"There's a fireplace in that bedroom. Come looky here, Wisteria!" I yelled.

"That living room has big old columns holding up the ceiling."

"Wow, look at those tall, winding stairs."

In the middle of all of Wisteria's and my hollering, we heard screaming coming from some place else, getting closer and closer. We looked up and saw Miss Eulalee running—well, shuffling her feet real fast—toward us, her hands on her cheeks, her great big old pillowy bosoms bouncing up and down.

"Help! Oh, help!" she shrieked, her cheeks flushed crimson.

Luke and Buddy rushed to her, and Buddy said, "What's the matter, Miss Eulalee? You look like you've seen a ghost."

"Queen Elizabeth!" she gasped.

"What about Queen Elizabeth?" Luke asked.

"She's gone. Just gone. Queen Elizabeth has never set paw outside my home, and now she is gone. Oh, who would do such a thing? Help! Oh, please help me!"

Then Miss Eulalee fainted dead away. Luke and Buddy grabbed her just before she hit the ground.

Buddy said, "Y'all stay here with Miss Eulalee while I go get Doc Spivey," and he took off in his truck toward Main Street and Doc Spivey's house.

He was back with the only doctor in town in less than ten minutes. By that time Miss Eulalee had come around and commenced to weeping over Queen Elizabeth. Doc checked her over, claimed she was just overwrought, and had Buddy drive him and Miss Eulalee back to her B&B, where he could fix her some tea and calm her down.

Sheriff Roudebush took a statement from Miss Eulalee but didn't get one step closer to cracking the case of the missing pets than he had before. The situation remained a complete bafflement.

* * *

Word spread like crazy because it always does in Lovington. First Chirpy and Lord Poodle, and then Larue, Miss Evaline's Rhode Island Reds, and now Queen Elizabeth.

"What is this damn town coming to?" Wisteria swore.

Luke said, "Stop that swearing, Wisteria. You know Mama doesn't like it when you swear. And don't you tell me you're just quotin' Papa Luke 'cause he doesn't have a thing to do with this."

"Calm down, Luke," Wisteria said, "even you gotta agree this situation lends itself to cussin'."

Luke just rolled his eyes, all exasperated with his little sister.

We were mighty glad we'd taken to penning up Kitty on the screened back porch to keep him safe from somebody with the M.O. of stealing the local pets.

Next morning Wisteria and I were in The Quilt Shop when Palmer Lee came hurrying in the store and charged right to the back without even speaking to Mama or Miss Nelda.

"Do y'all know what's going on? We went off yesterday for Daddy to do some hand shaking, and when we got back into town, there was a sign on the front door of the B&B that said, *Due to a bereft innkeeper, breakfast will not be served until further notice.* When Mama went looking for Miss Eulalee, she found a note on her bedroom door that said, *In mourning. Please do not disturb.* We didn't even realize Miss Eulalee had any family. Can y'all tell me what happened?"

"Sure can," said Wisteria, all of a sudden anxious to talk to Purdy Boy. "Seems like our pet stealer is at it again. He's done took off with Queen Elizabeth."

"You mean that big black and white cat that Miss Eulalee lets walk across her kitchen counter and sleep on the dining table?"

"That's the one," Wisteria told him.

"What a shame," said Palmer Lee, but he didn't seem too upset to be rid of a cat that walked where his food was being prepared and slept where he ate his breakfast. "I'm sorry for her loss, but I'm glad the lodge will be ready soon and we can have our own beds to sleep in. I'm getting right tired of Miss Eulalee's B&B."

"And her famous French toast casserole?" I asked.

"Yeah, and her famous French toast casserole," Palmer Lee said, and we all laughed, even Wisteria.

EIGHTEEN

Wisteria Hates
Damn Sissies!

Next day when Palmer Lee came into the shop, Wisteria said, "Hey, Purdy Boy, got any cats walking in your breakfast?"

Palmer Lee laughed and so did I, but only where nobody else could hear us.

"Miss Eulalee still won't come out of her room. Poor thing must really be upset," said Palmer Lee. "Does the sheriff have any idea who is responsible?"

"Not yet. He came in here this morning, asking me and Wisteria more questions, but we've already told him everything we know."

Then he said to me, "Let's go get a Cherry Coke. I want to tell you something."

I looked at Wisteria and saw that she was squinching her eyes at me. Then she turned real quick and started flinging around Miss Hilda Gooch's smocked baby bonnets.

"Sure," I said to Palmer Lee, "just let me tell Mama where I'm going." Then I said, "I won't be long, Wisteria."

She didn't look up from her flinging.

"Mama, me and Palmer Lee are going down to Uncle Ted's for a Cherry Co-Cola."

"Okay, honey, but hurry back."

"Yes, ma'am."

When we got to Uncle Ted's, Palmer Lee opened the door for me, as usual. He was such a gentlemen.

When Selma saw us come in, she yelled over at Uncle Ted, "On the house, Ted?"

"Right, Selma," was all he said, without even looking up from filling his prescriptions.

"Two Cherry Co-Colas, please," I said.

"Make that three, one of them to go," Palmer Lee told Selma. Then to me he said, "Let's take one to Wisteria."

I thought that was awful thoughtful of Palmer Lee, seeing as how Wisteria was being so rude to him. And seeing as how she wouldn't accept or even acknowledge his gifts anyway.

While we were drinking our Cherry Co-Colas, Palmer Lee said, "The lodge is all done. We're going to sleep up there tonight. Want to come up and see? It looks real good."

"Sure, I'd love to."

"Great!" Palmer Lee said. "I'll stop by and get you around seven."

Hmmm, tonight. I was supposed to have supper up at Wisteria's house. Her mama was fixing squirrel with cream gravy. Again. As I've said, many times, squirrel with cream gravy is not my favorite, but I can tolerate it just to make Wisteria happy. After supper we were planning to have a sleepover on her pull-out sofa in the living room. We were going to stay up late and make Chex Mix and watch TV after everybody else was in bed.

But Wisteria and I could have sleepovers and make Chex Mix and watch TV any old time. But it wasn't every night Palmer Lee Compton invited me up to see his senator-daddy's hunting lodge. Wisteria would just have to understand.

After we finished our drinks, I picked up Wisteria's Cherry Co-Cola and a couple of straws, and we headed on back to The Quilt Shop. At the door to the shop, Palmer Lee reached over and took my hand and squeezed it.

He smiled and said, "See you at seven," and he walked on off, leaving me feeling all warm inside.

When I walked in the store, Wisteria was waiting for me.

"I thought you'd never get back. We got work to do."

"Wisteria, I have a right to take a break every once in a while!" I said, real exasperated.

She huffed at me.

I was getting really tired of the way she was acting like such a baby, so I said to her, "Come on outside. I need to talk to you."

She followed me out the door, and we sat on the bench in front of the store. I could tell she was still upset at me for going off to Uncle Ted's with Palmer Lee. Her face was pinched all tight, and she wouldn't even look at me. Her feet didn't touch the sidewalk, and she was banging her orange high-tops together.

"Here, Palmer Lee sent you this," I said as I handed over her drink.

"Thanks," was all she said, taking it from me without looking me in the eye.

"Wisteria, you gotta stop acting this way. If I want to like Palmer Lee, I have every right to like him."

"All's I'm saying, Bit, is you better be careful. Mark my words, that Palmer Lee Compton is up to no good."

"So this isn't all about you being mad at me for liking a boy or scared that I'm gonna like him more than I like you?"

"Well, I'll admit, some of it is about that, but just think about it, Bit. He's a big city boy who goes to some highfalutin private school.

He could have any girl he wanted. What's he want with a little country girl like you? He's gonna hurt you, Bit. I can feel it in my bones."

"Stop it, Wisteria! That's not true. He likes me. I know he does."

"Oh, come on, Bit. He just doesn't have anything better to do while he's up here in the sticks with all us hicks than to hang around with you. Why, he can't even call his precious Trey and Tandy, back in big old Raleigh."

"Now, that was just mean, real mean, Wisteria!" I said, so angry, tears were starting to sting my eyes. "Take that back, right now!"

"Sorry, Bit, but you think about it. You know it's true."

Then the tears spilled over, and I started to cry.

I was so mad at her for saying those things about Palmer Lee and for acting like such a baby and for making me cry, so while I was blubbering, I blurted out, "And I can't have a sleepover with you tonight 'cause Palmer Lee has invited me up to see his daddy's hunting lodge."

Wisteria looked like I had slapped her. She got real red in the face, and she jumped up and screamed, "One of these days I'm gonna have me a boyfriend too, and I won't need no boobs to get him. I'm gonna use my brain!"

I just cried harder.

"Damn sissy, that's what you are," she said, the tears starting to come in her eyes too. "Just a damn sissy! And you know what I think of damn sissies! And I don't want Purdy Boy's damn Cherry Co-Cola neither!" she screamed and flang it on the sidewalk, splashing it all over my white tennis shoes and my legs. Then I watched her orange high-tops run like the wind up the street and disappear into a crowd of surprised-looking yella-headed ladies.

Once I couldn't see her anymore, I sat on the bench until my crying stopped good enough to go back inside. I raked my arm across my eyes and stood up, looking up the street one more time to see if Wisteria had decided to come back. She hadn't. I couldn't clean up the mess Wisteria had made on the sidewalk, but I did pick up her empty cup and turned to head back into the shop.

"Go get cleaned up," Mama said and took the cup from my hand.

She must have seen through the window what had happened between me and Wisteria.

I went all the way back to the bathroom and shut and latched the door. I sat down on the toilet and cried some more.

Pretty soon Mama pecked on the door and said, "Bit, you okay?"

I flipped the latch, and Mama came on in and closed the door behind her.

"What happened?"

I told her about Palmer Lee inviting me up to see his daddy's lodge and about telling Wisteria I couldn't have a sleepover and about Wisteria getting all mad, and she said, "Bit, Wisteria is your best friend, and you've hurt her feelings. You'll just have to be patient and understand what she's going through."

"But, Mama, it's not fair. If she had a boyfriend, I wouldn't be acting like such a big baby."

"You don't know that, Bit, 'cause that's never happened to you. Now wipe your face and clean yourself up. You need to get back to work. And since Wisteria is off licking her wounds, you're going to have to work twice as hard."

NINETEEN

Palmer Lee Shows
Bit the Hunting Lodge...
and a Whole Lot More

Palmer Lee came by at seven to get me. Mama and Daddy weren't real keen on me going out with a boy at night, but since we were just going up the holler road to see Palmer Lee's daddy's hunting lodge, they said it was okay, just this once.

"Palmer Lee," my daddy said, "you need to be getting Bit home before dark, you hear, son?"

"Yes, sir, I understand, Mr. Sizemore," Palmer Lee said, polite, like always. "Mama and Daddy said, 'Hello,' and they asked me to tell you that they want you to come up and take a look at the hunting lodge real soon. Mama wants you to see where she's put your quilts, Mrs. Sizemore."

"Thank you, Palmer Lee. That's awful nice. Tell your parents we'd love to."

Walking up the holler road, Palmer Lee took ahold of my hand. It felt good. He reached over and smoothed my hair away from my face. Then he leaned in and kissed me real sweet and soft, like he always did when we had a chance to be all alone, which wasn't very often.

When we passed Wisteria's house, I noticed she was swinging on the porch swing. NaCl was sitting by her side with her head resting on Wisteria's leg. Since we were so mad with each other, I didn't call out to her. When she saw me, she didn't say anything either, just got up and went inside, slamming the door real hard, leaving NaCl swinging all by herself, looking confused.

When we finally came to the spot in the holler road where Mose Beemus's house used to be, I screamed, "Good lord!"

I'm sure that if Wisteria had been with us, she'd have screamed, "Sweet baby Jesus on a June bug!" or "Yikes!"

I was used to seeing Mose's little old rickety shack, the yard all full of weeds and brambles and sticks and rocks. But Mose's house had been torn down and carted away to some place else, and there wasn't anything left but an empty lot that had been planted over with real green grass and pretty bushes and flowers. And right across the road from where Mose's little house used to be stood the grandest house I'd ever laid eyes on. It was humongous, and it was made out of great big stones, and it had lots of real tall windows. The yard was laid with bright green grass that looked like somebody had come in and rolled out a carpet, and the gardens were full of pink and white rhododendrons and mountain laurels and big, blue hydrangeas. There were yellow butterfly bushes on both sides of the stone sidewalk, and they were covered with blue and red and brown and yellow butterflies. I could hear bees buzzing around all those flowers, and the birds were chirping in the trees, like they were the happiest they'd ever been. They must have thought Senator Compton's lodge was just as amazing as I did. And over to one side of the yard was a great big swimming pool full of bright, blue water, with a diving board and a slide.

"There's a tennis court and shooting range out back," Palmer Lee told me, "and Wisteria is welcome to come and practice any time she likes."

"I'll tell her you said so."

"Want to see?"

"Sure, I'd love to."

He was still holding my hand as he led me past the pool, into the back yard. I couldn't believe my eyes. I hadn't ever seen anything like this, not even in magazines. The tennis court was out in the middle of bright, green grass, and the shooting range was off a ways, down by a big wooded area with lots of huge pine trees.

"Oh, Palmer Lee, I haven't ever seen anything as beautiful as this, not even over at the governor's mansion."

That's when he turned to me and smiled real sweet and said, "I'm so glad I met you this summer. You're so nice...and beautiful, really beautiful."

I didn't know what to say back 'cause nobody had ever called me beautiful before. Then he put his arms around me and kissed me. I liked kissing Palmer Lee because he smelled so good, like Dial soap, instead of all sweaty like most of the boys I knew. And his hands were real soft and smooth, without a single blister or callus on them. Then he pulled me in closer to him and did something he'd never done before. He stuck his tongue, gentle-like, in my mouth. And I liked that too. His tongue was real soft against my tongue, and he tasted nice, like Wrigley's Spearmint gum.

When we stopped kissing, Palmer Lee smiled real sweet at me and smoothed my hair away from my face again and made me tingle all over. I'd never felt like that before.

I didn't want him to stop kissing me, but he said, "Wait till you see inside."

He took my hand and walked me around to the front of the house and opened the great big, shiny wooden door and said, "Come on in."

The first thing I saw was the fireplace. It was made out of the same big stones as the outside of the house, and it went all the way to the ceiling, which was at least two stories high. And the opening where you built the fire was huge, taller than me.

So I ran over, hopped up on the raised hearth, and stood inside the fireplace. "Palmer Lee, look! I can't believe it. It's bigger than me."

Palmer Lee laughed and said, "Oh, Bit, you're so funny."

And while I was standing there in that great big fireplace with Palmer Lee looking at me, something Wisteria said to me earlier that day came back to me. Why would Palmer Lee want me when he could have any girl he wanted? And he was being with me just because there wasn't anything better to do. Sure, he said all the right things, but it's easy to say what people want to hear. It had sounded so mean when Wisteria said it, but for some reason, right then and there, it all started making sense.

I was just a little country girl who couldn't even dream a house as beautiful as the one I was standing in. And this was just the Comptons' play house, not even their real house. I hadn't been outside Lovington except on two school field trips and one piano competition over to the Capital and to Myrtle Beach on vacations with my mama and my daddy and Buddy. I didn't even know how to play tennis or golf like Palmer Lee and all his friends, and I sure hadn't ever been inside a country club. Most of all, I just went to a regular old school, not some fancy private school like Palmer Lee.

And Senator Compton had a play house with a fireplace that was taller than me.

Then I noticed something strange. It was real quiet in the house.

"Where are your mama and daddy?" I asked.

"Oh, they're at some political dinner down at the county seat. Daddy doesn't miss a chance to shake a hand, you know."

"But, Palmer Lee, I'm not allowed to be alone with a boy. That's like dating, and I already told you I can't date until I'm sixteen."

"Oh, Bit, it's no big deal. This isn't a date. I'm just going to show you around. I want you to see your mama's quilts. They look beautiful on our beds. Come on," he said, smiling and grabbing ahold of my hand.

He ran up the big steps, me trailing behind, trying to keep up. He was still clinging tight to my hand, like he was, all of a sudden, afraid I'd get away.

Once we got upstairs, the first rooms he took me to were the places for the guests to sleep, the important politicians and rich voters who would come up to the holler with Senator Compton on hunting trips. Each bed was covered with a quilt that Mama or Miss Nelda or one of the other quilt-club ladies had made. They were all a little different, but each one looked beautiful in Senator Compton's guest bedrooms.

Then Palmer Lee took me to his parents' room. It was so amazing I could hardly find any words to go along with what I was seeing. The furniture was made out of real dark wood, and it was huge, bigger than any furniture I'd ever laid eyes on, and it all fit Senator and Mrs. Compton's great big bedroom perfectly.

"This is so beautiful, Palmer Lee. Your mama did a wonderful job of decorating," I told him, not really knowing what to say. I still didn't feel right that I was alone with Palmer Lee, and I kept remembering what Wisteria had said.

"Some craftsman in Blowing Rock made all the furniture for Daddy and Mama just to fit this room. And Mama had help from a professional decorator, of course."

"Of course," I said. "It's really nice."

"I knew you'd like it. And look at your mama's quilt. Doesn't it look perfect on Mama and Daddy's bed?"

And there on Senator and Mrs. Compton's king-size bed was Mama's chained nine-patch quilt in rose, green, and teal. And Palmer Lee was right; it really was beautiful.

And I said, "If it hadn't been for my mama's quilts, none of this would have happened. Your daddy would never have brought your mama up to Lovington to see Mama's quilts, and he would never have built this beautiful lodge."

And Palmer Lee said, "And I'd have never met you, Bit."

He said that in a different sort of way than he normally talked, but I just couldn't quite put my finger on what was different about it. But that difference gave me a scary feeling real deep in my stomach.

I was sort of shaking when he took me down the hall, still holding onto my hand, to the last bedroom—Palmer Lee's. It wasn't as pretty as his mama and daddy's, but it was real nice. He had hand-made furniture, too, just to fit his room. And one of Mama's quilts, a green, blue, and red log-cabin design, was on his bed.

"It's really nice, Palmer Lee," I said, getting more jittery by the minute. "I think I better be going."

"What's your hurry?" he said, taking both my hands in his and rubbing my palms with his thumbs. "Your mama and daddy said you had to be home before dark. We have plenty of time."

"I know that, Palmer Lee, but..." Before I could finish, he pulled me close and kissed me, touching his tongue against my tongue again. I still liked kissing Palmer Lee, still liked that tingly feeling it gave me. But kissing Palmer Lee all alone in his bedroom scared me, and I knew I had to stop and get on home right then and there.

And I couldn't stop thinking about what Wisteria had said, that Palmer Lee only wanted to be with me because he didn't have anything better to do.

"I can't stay, Palmer Lee. Really, I gotta go," I said, trying to pull myself away from his hold on me.

"No you don't, Bit. We have time," he said, moving his lips down to my neck and holding me real tight.

"Stop it, Palmer Lee. I really, really gotta go."

Still holding onto me and breathing real hard into my neck, he said, "Oh, come on, Bit. Just stay. Stay a little. A little while."

His breath was ragged, and his words didn't make real good sense anymore, and his voice didn't even sound like Palmer Lee's.

Then when I tried to push him away, he held me tighter. No matter how hard I tried, I just couldn't break free of him. I was feeling scared and so guilty that I'd stayed in the house with Palmer Lee, especially after I'd found out that we were alone. And then I was crying and blubbering, and my mind was racing and wondering what was going on and how I was gonna get out of there.

That's when I knew, for sure, really sure, that Wisteria was right.

I screamed, "Stop it, Palmer Lee! Let me go!"

Palmer Lee sneered at me and said, "Let you go? Why, you ought to be glad I'd give you the time of day. You live up here in these back woods, all ignorant. You're nothing but a little know-nothing, ignorant hick!"

First off, I know I live in the back woods, and I didn't mind being called a hick. But one thing I did mind being called is ignorant. 'Cause I am not ignorant. And Palmer Lee calling me ignorant just made me real, real mad. So while he was still sneering at me, I pulled my arm free, balled up my fist, reared back, and clocked him right on the bridge of his nose.

Well, that sure made him let go of me. He crumpled to the floor and rolled around, holding his nose. I could see the blood seeping from underneath his hands. I must have gotten him directly in the right spot.

While Palmer Lee was nursing his busted nose, I screamed, "Guess they don't teach you over at that fancy school of yours that you shouldn't mess with a country hick girl with a big brother who's taught her how to defend herself."

Before I turned to run, I added, "And, by the way, there's nothing ignorant about me!"

TWENTY

Bit Sizemore Wants
Her Little Girl Back

I know all the paths through the woods, so I took off running toward home. I didn't take the holler road, because I was afraid Palmer Lee would follow me. I also figured it wouldn't take me as long to get home if I cut through the woods, and he would never think to come looking for me there. That's because Palmer Lee was a purdy city boy, and purdy city boys don't know the woods like us country-hick holler kids.

I ran fast as I could, jumping over downed trunks and dodging trees, and I didn't stop for anything until I reached our front yard. There I hid behind Kitty's sycamore tree until I could catch my breath and calm down. I didn't want Mama and Daddy to see me all frazzled and out of breath and start asking questions.

Kitty woke up and saw me, so he groaned as he got up and came over to give me a lick on my hand. I needed some comfort real bad, so I sank to the ground by that tree and wrapped my arms around my good old dog and held on tight. I was shaking real bad, so I hung on until I was calmed down and could ease up on my clutching. And right there behind that tree, while I was hanging onto my dog for comfort, was where I came to realize a whole bunch of stuff.

First off, I realized this was something I couldn't tell Mama, and I didn't like the feeling of that one little bit. I've done stupid stuff before that I haven't wanted Mama to find out about, but this was something altogether different. I didn't think I'd done anything wrong, but still I had a sorta guilty feeling. I had gone up to Palmer Lee's house, and I'd stayed alone with him even after I'd found out his mama and daddy weren't there. And, for some reason, I was feeling real shameful about that.

I also realized that somebody I liked and trusted a whole lot wasn't at all what I thought he was. Wisteria had told me to be careful and tried to warn me that Palmer Lee was gonna hurt me, but I wouldn't listen. It made me mad when she said that, and I didn't want it to be so. But it was all true.

Worst of all, I realized I wasn't a little girl any more. I wasn't quite sure why, but something about what Palmer Lee had done to me told me that very thing. I had always thought that when I stopped being a little girl, it would be a fun time—something to remember, something to share with my mama. But there was nothing fun about what had happened.

Once I'd calmed down, I patted Kitty on the head one last time and gave him a kiss between his eyes.

Then I said, "Come on, Kitty, we need to get you safe on the screened porch where nobody can hurt you."

I couldn't take somebody hurting my Kitty, especially after what I'd just been through.

So Kitty followed me to the back of the house and didn't complain when I locked him on the porch. He just plopped down in a heap, smacked his lips, and drifted off to sleep. I went on in the kitchen door and called out for Mama.

"Mama, I'm home."

"In here, sweetie," she called back.

I found Mama sitting in the living room, putting some finishing touches on one of her quilts.

She looked up from her sewing and smiled at me. I was surprised to see that her smile was the same one she gave me before I'd gone off with Palmer Lee. For some reason, I felt changed and expected everything else to be changed too. I was relieved to see that Mama's smile hadn't changed, though. I don't think I could've stood that, Mama's smile changing, on top of everything else.

"Hey, darlin', what'cha doing home so early?"

"Well, it didn't take long to look at Senator Compton's house."

"How are Senator and Mrs. Compton?"

"Fine, I guess."

"Didn't you talk to them?" she asked, looking at me kinda quizzical-like.

"No, ma'am, they were busy with some voters, shaking hands and stuff, you know."

It wasn't a lie. But it wasn't quite the truth either.

So to change the subject, I said, "Mama, your quilts look real pretty in Senator Compton's lodge."

"Oh, good, I can't wait to see them," she said. Then she asked, "Where's Palmer Lee?"

"He went on back home. Guess his mama and daddy didn't want him out after dark either."

Before she could ask any more questions, I said, "I think I'm gonna go to my room and read."

And Mama said, "Okay, sweetie," and went on back to her sewing.

I wondered how she could just go on back to what she was doing, like nothing had happened at all. Then I realized that she didn't know that Palmer Lee had scared me and hurt my feelings so bad. But how could she not know? I was her little girl. Mamas are supposed to know these things. That was so confusing. I didn't want to tell her, but, somehow, I expected her to already know. Is that what it's like when you stop being a little girl? It makes you go all crazy in your mind and makes your thoughts fuzz up?

I decided right then and there I wanted my little girl back.

I dropped my clothes on the floor and kicked my shoes under the bed, then put on my pajamas. I climbed into bed and picked up my library book from the bedside table. I was still working on *The Outsiders*.

I found my place and tried to read.

But the words wouldn't go past my eyes. My brain was so full of angriness and scaredness and confusion and sorrow, that the words just couldn't get in. I was still sitting there, the words slamming up against my eyes, when Mama came in to kiss me good-night.

"Night, darlin'," she said and kissed me on my forehead, "Don't stay up too late. And sleep tight."

When she left, I kept on staring at the words, but since they didn't mean anything, I just put my book away and turned out the light. I lay there with my eyes open and watched the dark. And I was still watching the dark when it turned to light. I finally got up, put my clothes back on, and crawled under the bed for my shoes. Then I went to the bathroom and washed my face and brushed my teeth and pulled my hair back into a ponytail.

When I went downstairs, I saw Mama cooking breakfast and Daddy sitting at the kitchen table, drinking his coffee and reading the paper.

"Where's Buddy?" I asked.

"Giving him the day off," Daddy said. "He's been working hard for me. He and Luke are going to the river to do a little fishing this morning."

Mama said. "How about some pancakes?"

"No, thanks, Mama, I think I'll just have some toast."

Daddy looked up from reading his paper and said, "That doesn't sound like much breakfast for a growing gal."

"Not too hungry. Just some toast, with maybe a little apple butter."

So I got two slices of bread from the loaf and dropped them in the toaster and waited. When they popped up, I smeared a little of Mama's homemade apple butter on each slice, put them on a plate, and took it to the table.

"Juice?" Mama asked.

"Sure. Thanks, Mama."

I nibbled for a while, pretending I was eating, but I didn't have any appetite at all. When Mama and Daddy started talking to each other and weren't paying me any attention, I slipped over and stuffed the remains of my toast in the disposal and turned it on. Then I rinsed my plate and put it in the dishwasher.

"I'm gonna go call Wisteria," I said.

"Okay, darlin'," Mama said and kept on talking to Daddy.

Miss Faylene answered the phone.

"Miss Faylene, this is Bit. May I please speak to Wisteria?"

"Jus' sec, honey."

She was gone a good long while before she came back. "Bit, honey, Wisteria can't come to the phone right now. But I'll tell her you called."

I put down the phone and said, "Mama, I'm going up to Wisteria's. I'll be a little late getting to the store. Is that okay?"

Mama was rinsing her and Daddy's breakfast dishes and loading them in the dishwasher. She turned off the faucet, dried her hands on her apron, and came over to me.

She put her hand on my cheek and said, "Darlin', healing this pain between you and Wisteria is far more important than you stocking shelves. Here, take these to Wisteria," she said, reaching into the cookie jar and grabbing a handful of goin'-to-school cookies. She dropped them in a paper sack and handed it to me. Kissing me on the cheek, she said, "Bit, I can see the hurt in your eyes. I hope you and Wisteria can work things out."

There was hurt in my eyes, all right, and my heart, too, and in every other part of my body. But my sweet mama had no idea why I was in so much pain. She never would know. I hated keeping that awful truth from her, but I was so ashamed, so hurt and embarrassed that I had believed a rich pretty boy from the big city could have been interested in me. And, yes, I was so sorry that I had hurt my best friend over some silly, sweet-talking purdy boy.

I kissed Mama back and headed out the kitchen door. When he saw me, Kitty got up on his old creaky legs, stretched real long, and trotted out the screen door beside me.

When we got up to Wisteria's house, there wasn't a soul in sight, so I knocked on the door. I had a pretty long wait before Wisteria answered. She didn't say a word, just stared up at me in a sorrowful sort of way.

"You were right."

"I know."

"He hurt me."

"Yeah," was all she said.

"Can we go to the pond. I need to talk real bad."

"Sure," she said, stepping out and closing the door, not even bothering to tell Miss Faylene she was leaving.

All she was thinking about was me.

While we were walking, I handed her the sack of cookies. "Mama sent you these."

"That was nice. I just had my breakfast, so I'll save 'em till later."

When we got to the pond, we walked to the end of the dock and sat down. I took off my tennis shoes and dangled my feet in the water. It was still early in the morning and the sun hadn't crested the trees, so the water was right cool. It felt good.

Wisteria sat down beside me, crossed her legs, and waited for me to talk.

Kitty plopped down beside me, sighed, and put his head on my leg.

I took a deep breath and looked out over the pond. The fog was sitting right on top of the water, looking kinda like the angel hair that Buddy and I had put on the Christmas tree when we were little tiny kids. Mama stopped buying it for us, though, 'cause turns out the stuff had fiberglass in it, and it cut Buddy's and my hands something awful.

"He said mean things. Called me mean names."

Wisteria didn't say anything for the longest time, so I looked sideways at her just in time to see a big old tear slide down her cheek. She brushed it away with the back of her hand, but she didn't call herself a *damn sissy*.

What she did say was, "I'll kick that purdy boy's sorry ass."

Usually I'd laugh or ask if she was just quotin', but I was in no laughing or joking mood.

Instead, I put my face in my hands to cover my shame and said, "Oh, Wisteria, I was a stupid idiot to think some big-city boy could like a little hick girl like me. I'm so ashamed. I was just asking for it."

When I said that, Wisteria jumped up, balled her fists at her sides, and screamed at me, "You stop that right now! You hear me, Bit? Stop it! No girl asks to be mistreated. You didn't do anything wrong, besides trusting a sweet-talking, sorry-ass purdy boy."

"But why do I feel so guilty, Wisteria?"

Sitting back down and crossing her legs and scootching real close to me, she said, "'Cause there's people who try to make girls feel guilty, that's why. They say, 'You sent the wrong message,' or 'If you hadn't put yourself in that situation, it would never have happened.' Bit, maybe you shouldn't have been in that house alone with that boy when you knew your mama and daddy didn't want you to be there. But that's all you did wrong. All! You understand? He did wrong, not you."

I thought about what she said for a long time, then said, "You're so smart, Wisteria."

"Yeah, I know. That's one of the things I brought to our friendship. Remember?"

"Yeah, I remember."

But I had done something very wrong. Real wrong. I had hurt my best friend so bad. I had made her cry like a damn sissy, the thing she hated most in all the world. But she didn't remind me of that, didn't even say, "I told you so."

She opened her sack and said, "Here, have a goin'-to-school cookie."

"No, thanks. I'm not in a goin'-to-school-cookie mood."

So we just sat there for the longest time, looking out over the pond and not eating cookies.

"Wisteria," I said, "don't you ever wish you could go back to playing dolls and having your mama sit on your bed with you at night and read you a story?"

"Nah," she answered, not looking at me, "I've never been one to play with dolls. And I never did need for Mama to sit on my bed and read me a story. I could read to myself."

"Oh," was all I could think to say, sad that Wisteria never liked dolls and sadder still that her mama had never read her a bedtime story.

Finally Wisteria said, "We gotta get to work."

The sun was rising. The fog was lifting. The water was getting warm on my feet. I reached into Wisteria's sack and grabbed a goin'-to-school cookie.

I took a bite and said, "Wisteria, I hit him square in the nose. It bled real bad. Betcha he'll have a black eye by tomorrow."

Wisteria reached in and took a cookie and bit into it and thought for a minute about what I'd said.

"So what you're saying is you don't need for me to kick his sorry ass 'cause you already did that."

We both started laughing as I put my shoes back on. We stood up and headed down the dock to the holler road on our way to work.

When we passed my house, I said, "Kitty, you go on home now."

He looked up at me with a face full of love and then trotted on off to his sycamore tree. He looked back at me once before he settled into his puddle of fur and sighed before closing his eyes. I still say Kitty was a really smart old dog.

The day was pretty uneventful. Same yella-headed ladies tromped in and out, some of them bringing their decorators to help them pick out stuff for their new vacation homes down by the river. We had two tour buses—a bunch of folks coming to spend the morning shopping before going over to the bypass to have lunch at McDonald's or Taco Bell.

Mrs. Compton came in to pick up some pillow shams that one of Mama's quilt-club friends had made for her. Palmer Lee was not with her.

Mrs. Compton said, "Morning, Bit," and acted like she didn't have any idea I'd even been up to her and Senator Compton's lodge the night before.

And I sure didn't mention it.

When noon came, Wisteria and I went back to the storage room and found the bread and peanut butter that Mama kept back there so Wisteria and I could have a snack when we got hungry. Since we'd gone to the pond instead of packing a lunch, we fixed ourselves a peanut butter sandwich and got a cup of water from the fountain by the restroom. Then we took it out to the bench in front of the store.

Wisteria took a bite of her sandwich and asked, "You okay?"

I told her I thought I was but that I wasn't quite sure.

"Well, you'll be fine tomorrow 'cause the Fall Is Just Around the Corner Festival can cure anything, right?"

"Right, Wisteria," I said, not believing that at all.

"We are gonna have the best time, Bit. I have been counting down the days for about ninety days now. Hurry and finish your sandwich so we can get on back to work. We gotta finish tagging those baby dresses and cleaning the restroom. 'Cause we need to get on home and rest up for tomorrow."

TWENTY-ONE

Baptist Biscuit Booth and More at the Fall Is Just Around the Corner Festival

"You got your spending money?" I asked Wisteria when she showed up at the house the next day, an hour early.

"Sure do, I brought a bunch. Better to have too much than too little. Got it hidden in my orange high-top. Makes me walk a little lopsided, but I want to keep it safe and away from the prying eyes of strangers," she said, charging into the kitchen.

"If you're walking lopsided, then why don't you put half of your money in your left shoe and half of it in your right shoe?" I asked her.

Wisteria whacked herself on the forehead with the heel of her hand and said, "Well, duh! Why didn't I think of that? And I'm supposed to be the smart one," she said, cutting her eyes at me.

I just laughed.

"Hey, Wisteria," Mama said.

"Sorry to intrude on your breakfast, Miss Brenda, but I am beside myself with excitement. I have been waiting and planning for this moment for about three whole months."

"Well, I can certainly understand your excitement. The Fall Is Just Around the Corner Festival happens only once a year."

"Yes, ma'am, and, thanks to your generosity, I will be able to ride lots of rides, take in some side shows, eat plenty of midway food, and even play games of chance."

"Glad I could help, Wisteria. It sounds very exciting. Now grab yourself a bowl out of the cupboard there and fix yourself some cereal. You can't go to the festival on an empty stomach."

"Well, it's really not empty, Miss Brenda, since I already had me a biscuit with Mama's homemade peach preserves before I left the house, but I believe I could handle a bowl of Cheerios, if you can spare some."

"I can," Mama said and gave Wisteria a quick hug. "Right there in the pantry, sweetie, and grab a banana out of the fruit bowl."

"Well, thanks, Miss Brenda. Don't mind if I do."

We had just sat down with our cereal when Buddy came dragging in, sleep still in his eyes and his hair sticking out every which-a-way.

"Mornin', Itty Bitty. Hey, there, Cuteness," he said and tugged on Wisteria's braid.

Wisteria still didn't take kindly to folks tugging on her orange braids, but she made an exception for Buddy, especially when he called her Cuteness.

"Hey, Buddy," Mama said, "you'll have to get your own breakfast this morning. I have to get downtown. I need to open the store early. No telling how much business we'll be getting from all the festival folks. Will you take Bit and Wisteria down to the festival when you go?"

I started whining, "But, Mama, we can walk."

"I know that, darlin', but it's a long way and you're gonna want to spend the whole day in town. I don't want you girls worn out before your day even begins. Just ride on down with Buddy. Okay?"

"Yes, ma'am," I said, none too happy, but added, "thanks for giving me and Wisteria the day off."

"Well, that was our agreement when I hired you. Only summer hours since you feel your education is important and you need to go to school. No work that involves driving a car. And no Saturday work since you need your Saturdays free to work on your friendship."

"That's right, Mama, but you're gonna be awful busy because of all the festival people."

"A deal's a deal. No Saturday work. And, besides, Wisteria has been counting the days till the Fall Is Just Around the Corner Festival."

Then she winked at Wisteria.

"My mama's already down at the festival, Miss Brenda. She went at six o'clock this morning to help set up the Baptist Biscuit Booth and start making ham biscuits."

"That's nice that your mama is helping out at the Baptist booth, Wisteria. Those ham biscuits are the best thing on the midway. I may have to get you girls to bring me one over to the store."

"We'll be glad to do that, Miss Brenda," Wisteria told her.

"Okay, girls, y'all rinse out your bowls and put them in the dishwasher when you're through. And be careful down at that festival, you hear?"

"All right, Mama, we will."

I planned to be very careful and do exactly what I knew my mama and daddy wanted me to do. I'd had enough guilt and scaredness for a good, long while.

"Okay, girls," Buddy said after he'd tipped up his cereal bowl and drunk all the milk. "I'm gonna run take a quick shower, and then we'll head on down to the festival."

Before we could get the cereal bowls rinsed and put in the dishwasher, Buddy was back, wearing fresh jeans and a tee shirt, sporting wet comb tracks in his hair.

Mama and Daddy had given Buddy a big red Chevy truck for his sixteenth birthday, so he and Wisteria and I hopped in and went rumbling down the holler road. On the way, Wisteria took off her shoes and evened up her money so she wouldn't walk lopsided. When we got to Main Street, we saw that Mama had put the big sandwich board that said OPEN out on the sidewalk. Folks were already pouring in the door of The Quilt Shop, and I was hoping Mama and Miss Nelda could handle the crowds for one day without me and Wisteria.

I marveled at how much Lovington had changed over the summer. Uncle Ted's business was doing better than he ever dreamed, and when we drove by, we saw him unlocking the pharmacy door early, just to accommodate the festival folk.

Buddy tooted his horn and yelled out his open window, "Hey, Uncle Ted."

He turned and waved and called out, "Hey, kiddos. Y'all have fun today."

Mr. Carl, right next door to Uncle Ted's, was already wiping down his bistro tables and chairs and spreading out his red-checkered table cloths. It was a little early in the day for bistro dining, but those ladies shopping down at The Quilt Shop just might want to stop by for a cup of coffee or tea and a pastry on their way to the Fall Is Just Around the Corner Festival.

Mr. Wilson was opening Antiques and Junque early. Guess he figured the festival would be bringing him and Mr. Ralston lots of business, and he wanted to be ready. I believe it took a while before Mr. Wilson and Mr. Ralston could feel at home here in Lovington, what with busybody people like Miss Pearline spreading gossip about them being unnatural and all. But people have gotten over that pretty much, since everybody knows that Miss Pearline is just a lonely old lady who doesn't have anything better to do than cook Vi-enna sausage pastries and make up stories about people. And everybody has come to realize Mr. Wilson and Mr. Ralston are just real nice people, like everybody else. And all those yella-headed ladies want antiques and junque just as much as they want quilts.

Truth be told, the only thing people find unnatural about Mr. Wilson and Mr. Ralston these days is that they're vegetarians. They even invite folks up to their place and give them cooking lessons using nothing but vegetables and fruit and beans. They call the beans *legumes*. That must be the New York word for beans. They also cook tofu, something that looks nothing like meat but Mr. Wilson and Mr. Ralston say they can make taste like meat. Now, Lovington citizens have no intention of giving up eating meat, but they do accept Mr. Wilson and Mr. Ralston's invitations to their cooking classes out of pure curiosity.

And Wisteria pure-T loves to rummage through Mr. Wilson and Mr. Ralston's doodads and knick-knacks. She even used some of her festival money to buy herself that purple felt hat that comes all the way down to the tops of her eyes with the big green feather sticking out the side. It goes great with orange French braids and orange high-top tennis shoes. She had planned to wear her purple felt hat to the Fall Is Just Around the Corner Festival, but she was afraid she might lose it on one of the many exciting rides she planned to take.

And then there's Miss Dixie's shop. It used to be just the one little room with ladies' underthings and bathing suits and prom dresses and such till all craziness broke loose. That's when she decided to sign a lease on the old vacant Cato's store next door and cut a hole in the wall between the two stores. She even painted the front of her new, expanded building bright pink and put black and white striped awnings over the windows. It looks right nice, all spruced up like that. She put in a line of weekender clothes, lots of jeans and corduroy pants and flannel shirts and hats and rubber boots. Miss Dixie's business is booming. She's even had to hire a full-time bookkeeper.

Mr. Hammitt at the hardware store has had to take on two new workers, what with all those new vacation houses going in down by the river. Even with Home Depot over by the bypass, he's busier than he's ever been.

Doc Spivey keeps threatening to retire, but he can't when he's got so many patients, some of them just passing through, and he's the only doctor in Lovington. He's been talking to Buddy about going to college at the University over in Chapel Hill and then on to medical school so he can come back home and take over his medical practice. Buddy's real smart and is the president of everything down at Lovington High School, so he's thinking seriously about Doc Spivey's proposal.

And Miss Eulalie is tickled pink with her fine B&B. She's still overcome with grief over Queen Elizabeth's disappearance, but she's got herself a new Queen Elizabeth, Jr. that she allows to walk on the kitchen counter and sleep on the dining room table. And she doesn't let it out of her sight. Every morning she has reason to get up and put on one of her frilly organdy party dresses cut low on her powdery pillow bosoms, when she serves her guests her famous French toast casserole and fruit compote. She keeps her guest rooms full most all the time.

And then there's Miss O.O. over at the post office. She finally had to cry uncle and hire somebody to help her out—somebody old enough to take that civil service exam.

And there, about a block past O.O.'s post office and Mr. Fisher's filling station at the far end of Main Street was the Fall Is Right Around the Corner Festival.

Wisteria screamed, "Yikes!" when she saw it and dug into her shoes and pulled out her money to buy tickets for rides and tickets for sideshows and tickets for games of chance.

Buddy found a parking spot and said, "Now, y'all have fun. I'm gonna go find Luke, and we'll catch up with y'all later on. Remember, I owe you a stuffy."

First off we headed for the Tilt-A-Whirl. I like the Tilt-A-Whirl because it just goes round and round and doesn't leave the ground. I don't like leaving the ground. Being up high gives me the jitteries and makes my stomach come up in my throat. Then we rode on the merry-go-round. I love the merry-go-round, always have. I love the music, which is called calliope music, just like my best friend's middle name, Calliope. I also love the bright colors and all the beautiful painted animals. Everybody likes to ride on a big, tall horse, but I always ride on the swan. She—I think it's a she—is so beautiful and graceful. But the real reason I like to ride the swan is because it was Sondra's favorite thing to ride on the merry-go-round. And riding on the swan makes me think of Sondra—in a good sort of way, not in a bleeding-the-sorrow-out sort of way.

Next we headed for the Ferris wheel, which I do not like one bit. Like I said, being up high gives me the jitteries. But I make myself ride the Ferris wheel every year. That's 'cause when I was eight years old, Ricky Screven pushed me down and scraped my knees and made them bleed, and he called me a baby when I cried on the Ferris wheel. So every year I ride the Ferris wheel, and I hope that Ricky Screven sees me. I still don't like it, and I almost cry every time. But I don't. I don't think Ricky Screven has ever seen me ride the Ferris wheel since that day he pushed me down. But I'll keep trying. And I still have a scar on my knee from when he pushed me down that time.

"Okay, Wisteria, I've had enough rides. Now I want something to eat."

"Me too. I'm hungry," she said, even though she'd had a biscuit with homemade peach preserves and Cheerios with a banana for breakfast.

But eating was one of the things that brought us to the Fall Is Just Around the Corner Festival in the first place. And being hungry isn't the only reason you eat festival food. You eat it just because it's there. So we headed for the midway food vendors. I ate a funnel cake, and Wisteria had a sausage with peppers hoagie, a strawberry ice cream cone, and corn on the cob. I figured that little spindly thing was gonna have a belly ache for sure, but she was having the time of her life. She probably figured it was worth just one great big old belly ache to be able to eat anything she pleased.

Sucking the corn-on-the-cob butter off her fingers, she screamed, "Well, I'll be damn! Looky there!" pointing toward the sign that said *Whistling Contest.*

"You planning on entering the whistling contest?" I asked her.

"Ya think?" she said, grinning and pointing to the gap between her teeth.

"You'll just be wasting your time. Can't anybody beat Ray Boy Whetby."

"Who?"

"Ray Boy, Milo Whetby's boy."

"Who the heck is that?

"Well, the Whetbys live out in the country, west of Mount Pine. While back Mr. Milo had a five-legged cow. Don't know where that fifth leg came from. Daddy called it a freak of nature. They named it

Myrtle—the cow, not the leg. That fifth leg wasn't as big as the other four legs, and it wasn't good for walking or anything else, just for hanging there like a decoration."

"Whoa, that's weird!" Wisteria said.

"Yeah, it was pretty weird. But Myrtle was very protective of that do-nothing fifth leg, and she didn't cotton to anybody touching it. Mr. Milo's son, Ray Boy, though, was a real curious sort, and his curiosity made him want to grab ahold of Myrtle's fifth leg in the worst kind of way. Mr. Milo knew this about his son, so he told him, 'Now, Ray Boy, don't you be messing with Myrtle's do-nothing leg. You just leave her be. She don't like for nobody to be touching 'at thing.' But Ray Boy's curiosity got the best of him, so once he reached out and grabbed ahold of that do-nothing leg. When he did that, Myrtle twirled around, reared up her hind legs—the ones that worked—and kicked Ray Boy's front teeth clean out of his mouth. After that, every time Ray Boy tried to talk, he'd whistle through that big old gap that Myrtle had made when she kicked out his front teeth."

"Damn! Bet that hurt like the devil."

"Maybe so, but that's really not part of the story, Wisteria. The story is that every year Ray Boy comes to the Fall Is Just Around the Corner Festival just so he can enter the whistling contest. And with that big old gap between his teeth—which, by the way, is lots bigger than yours—nobody else has a chance at winning."

"Well, he hasn't met me yet, now, has he? I'm gonna give that Ray Boy Whetby a run for his money."

So Wisteria signed up and gave a real passable effort. But there's no beating Ray Boy. Once he gets wound up, he sounds like one of those plastic bird whistles we used to fill up with water and blow through in kindergarten.

Wisteria made a good enough showing that she came in a distant second. For her efforts the man handing out prizes gave her a Barbie Doll with a pink tutu and pink ballet slippers.

"Damn sissy," she mumbled when the announcer at the whistling contest gave it to her. "But I suspect Virginia and Faye would like it. Let's take it over to Mama and have her put it in her pocketbook to take home. I don't want to be toting this damn sissy thing around all day. And while we're there, maybe we can get us one of those Baptist biscuits."

"Didn't you have a biscuit for breakfast?"

"Yeah, but not a Baptist biscuit. That's a whole 'nother thing, Bit."

So Wisteria and I pushed our way through the crowd that was getting bigger by the minute and made our way over to the Baptist Biscuit Booth.

"Looky what I won in the whistling contest," Wisteria told her mama when we got to the Baptist Biscuit Booth.

"Well, congratulations, Wisteria!" Miss Faylene told her.

"Thanks, Mama, but I don't want that d... darn sissy thing." *Nice save, Wisteria.* "You think Faye and Virginia would like to play with it?"

"I'm sure they would, Wisteria. I'll hold on to it and take it home when I go."

"Thanks, Mama. While we're here, can we have three ham biscuits? Me and Bit want one, and we promised Miss Brenda we'd take her one over to The Quilt Shop."

"Why, sure, honey," Miss Faylene said. And then she added, "And they're my treat."

Miss Faylene put Mama's biscuit in a brown paper sack, and I stuck it in my pocket while she gave us our biscuits in wax paper wrappings.

"Thanks, Miss Faylene. That's awful nice. I'll tell Mama it was your treat."

"Thanks, Mama. I'll see you later," Wisteria said and turned to leave.

We ate our biscuits, the very best eating at the Fall Is Just Around the Corner Festival, if you ask me.

Then we wandered around the midway till Wisteria said, "I gotta pee."

I said, "That salty ham made me mighty thirsty, so while you're peeing, I'll go get us a Co-Cola."

"Okay. Then go wait for me over by the ring toss."

I'd gotten our Co-Colas and was standing by the ring toss, watching Benny Slattery waste all his money, when I felt a hand grab ahold of my arm and pull me between the ring toss booth and the floating-rubber-duck game. When I turned around, I saw that it was Palmer Lee Compton who had grabbed at my arm. The bridge of his nose was red and all swolt up, and both of his eyes had begun turning black.

"Let go of me, Palmer Lee," I said and tried to pull away from him.

But he was holding on tight, like he was desperate.

"I just want to talk to you, Bit," he said.

"No, I don't have anything to say to you, and I don't want to hear anything you have to say," I told him.

I sounded real brave, but I was shaking real hard on the inside.

"Please, Bit," he said, still holding on to me.

And even though my insides were shaking real hard, I looked him square in the eye and said, "Palmer Lee Compton, you gotta learn that when a girl says *no*, she means *no*! Now, let go of me."

From behind me I heard Wisteria say, "What happened to you, Purdy Boy? Did you slip in your fancy deck shoes and hit your face on your daddy's big old expensive Lexus?"

Palmer Lee's face turned red, about as red as his nose, and he let go of my arm, causing me to splash some of my Co-Cola—accidentally—

on his yellow shirt sleeve. He looked at me with a real I'm-sorry look on his face and just turned and walked away. Then he glanced back over his shoulder at me one more time before he disappeared into the crowd.

I handed Wisteria her Co-Cola, the one I hadn't accidently spilled on Palmer Lee's shirt, and we started walking down the midway. I couldn't get that sad look on Palmer Lee's face out of my mind. I'd never seen him look like that before.

"There y'all are! We've been looking all over for you."

We turned around and saw Buddy and Luke coming toward us.

"It's time for me to win you girls a stuffy over at the shooting range," Buddy said. "I'm gonna give old Luke here a shooting lesson."

Luke smiled that white-tooth grin of his. Where Buddy is sorta-blonde with big brown eyes, just like me, Luke has jet black hair and the palest blue eyes, kinda like Daddy Earl. He's real good looking, with the kind of looks that make girls have crushes on him.

Wisteria smiled a half-smile at Buddy and said, "You gonna win me one too?"

"Sure thing. Anybody named Cuteness has to have a stuffy, don't you think?" he said and put his arms around us both and walked us over to the shooting range.

Didn't take him long to win us each a stuffy, because Buddy's the best shot in all of Lovington—even better than Wisteria, but she would never admit it.

"What'll it be, girlies?" the man inside the booth asked.

I looked up at all the stuffed animals. I had most of them. And, to be real honest, I didn't have stuffies on my mind.

"There, that one," I said, kinda half interested. "I'll take the dolphin with the sailor's cap. I don't have that one."

"A dolphin for the pretty little lady," the man said.

He had a cigarette in the corner of his mouth, and he was squinching up one of his eyes to keep the smoke out of it. When he handed me my dolphin, I noticed that his pointy finger and middle finger were real yellow, I guessed from holding his cigarette when it wasn't stuck in the corner of his mouth. I also noticed that he was missing half of his ring and pinky fingers on his yellow-fingers hand. I wondered how he had cut off his fingers, and I felt right sorry for him. But he didn't seem to feel sorry for himself. He acted real happy to be giving stuffies to girlies.

"And what'll it be for you, little gal?" he said to Wisteria.

She didn't seem any more excited about stuffies than me, but she studied the shelf real hard, just the same. Guess she figured if Buddy was nice enough to win stuffies for us, she'd act real grateful about it.

"Since you don't have a Katy Perry, I think I'll take that horse up there, the one like Bit's, with the leatherette saddle and the blue and red rhinestones. I want the brown one, please."

"A brown horse for the little orange-haired cutie," said the man with the two yellow fingers and the two missing fingers.

"Thank you, sir," said Wisteria. "Thanks, Buddy," she said and gave him a hug.

"Thank you, Buddy," I said. Then I told him, "I'm tired. I think I'll go on home."

"Sure y'all don't want to go on some rides with us?" he asked.

"Thanks," I said, "but I believe we've done enough."

"Y'all want me to give you a ride home?"

"Nah, we're gonna walk down to The Quilt Shop before we go on home. We've got a Baptist biscuit for Mama," I said, pulling it out of my pocket to show him. "But thanks, anyway. And thanks for the stuffies."

We walked the length of Main Street, my dolphin under my arm, Wisteria's horse under hers, and we didn't say a word to each other the whole time. When we got to The Quilt Shop, Mama said we looked exhausted and asked if we wanted her to give us a ride home.

"No, ma'am. We just wanted to stop by and give you your biscuit. It was Miss Faylene's treat, by the way."

"Well, that was awful sweet of your mama, Wisteria. Please tell her I said thanks."

"Will do, Miss Brenda."

"Well, Mama, me and Wisteria are gonna walk on home."

She felt my head for fever and said, "If you're sure."

"Yes, ma'am, we're sure," we both said.

And Wisteria and I trudged toward the holler road and home.

TWENTY-TWO

Will Wisteria's
Hunch
Pay Off?

"Bit, did y'all have fun yesterday?" Daddy asked the next morning at the breakfast table.

"Yes, sir," I said, sort of half-way.

"I'm sorry I couldn't go with you kids. But the light fixtures came in for Mrs. McClelland's and Mrs. Batson's houses down by the river, and I needed to start installing them. 'Cause, as y'all know, they're both chomping at the bit to get in by fall.

"But, Harrison, we simply must be in before the leaves turn," Daddy said in a real high voice, batting his eyes and waving his hands in the air and pretending to act like the yella-headed ladies whose husbands were building them vacation houses down by the river.

We all laughed at Daddy's imitation.

"Okay, that's enough silliness for one Sunday morning," Daddy said. "Run feed your dog, Bit. We need to be getting ready for church or we're gonna be late."

"Yes, sir," I said and went in the pantry and dipped the beat-up old tin pot down into Kitty's fifty-pound sack of Jim Dandy dog food.

No fancy dog food with chicken and vegetables and such for Kitty. He just wanted that old dry stuff he could come back to all day and crunch to his heart's delight with the few teeth he had left for crunching. I carried it out to the back porch to dump into his big old chipped earthenware dinner bowl.

I remember dropping the pot of dog food and seeing it spray high in the air and land all over the porch, but I don't remember me screaming.

But I do recall Daddy grabbing me up and yelling, "What in the world is wrong, Bit?"

"Look, Daddy," I said, pointing to the screen door.

Someone had apparently yanked at the door so hard that it pulled the latch clean out.

And there was no sign of Kitty.

We didn't make it to church.

Daddy called Sheriff Roudebush, and he came right up and brought along Deputy Jerry.

"Any ideas yet?" Daddy asked.

"None, Harrison. You know, ever since Brenda and Nelda turned their hobby into a quilt store down there on Main Street, Lovington ain't been the same. Got strangers crawling all over the place. Could've been any one of 'em. Could have even been one of our own, all stirred up by the change."

"Wait a minute, Lonnie!" my daddy said, real angry-like. "You trying to say my wife is somehow responsible for the animals going missing?"

"Just saying, Harrison, Lovington is splitting at the seams since Brenda and Nelda and their quilts got so well known. I don't begrudge your wife her fame, so to speak, but it's just a fact of life. Change makes things happen. Good and bad. And when your pet dog gets kidnapped right off your own back porch, that's bad, Harrison, real bad."

"I know it's bad, Sheriff, but you were elected to hunt down the bad. What are you and Jerry going to do about it?"

"Wish I could do more than I'm doing, Harrison, but since the town has grown so fast the way it has, me and Jerry got just about more 'n we can handle. Maybe you and Ted and Double and the rest of the town council could be talking about getting me some more help."

"I'm sorry, Lonnie. You're right. You've taken on a lot lately. I'll bring it up at the next council meeting. But what do we do till then?"

"Guess we'll just have to keep locking up our animals where nobody can get to 'em and keep an eye out for folks lurking around at night."

"Well, that's not much comfort," Daddy said.

"Sorry, Harrison," Sheriff Roudebush said, hanging his head, kicking a stone around in the driveway with the toe of his boot. "Me and Jerry'll keep our eyes and ears open. That's about the best we can do. And we'll just have to ask all the citizens of Lovington to do the same."

Then the Sheriff and Jerry shuffled on back to their squad car, looking like they were all weighed down with woes, and headed on back to town without even solving a thing or acting like they were gonna be able to.

"Mama," I said, "can I call Wisteria and ask her to come down?"

"Sure, darlin'. First, though, go get some clothes on and brush your teeth. Then I think calling Wisteria to come down would be a real good idea."

After I'd done what Mama said, I called up to Wisteria's house.

"Wisteria," I said and started crying real hard.

Without asking what was wrong or calling me a damn sissy, she said, "I'll be right there. I'll tell Mama I can't go to Sunday school. My best friend crying trumps Sunday school any old day."

She was there in about fifteen minutes, her face all pink and sweaty from running all the way in her magic orange high-tops. It didn't matter to her that she wasn't supposed to be my Sunday friend.

I told her about Kitty being kidnapped, and while I cried my eyes out, she took to cussing under her breath. "Damn pansy. Damn coward. That was a damn fine dog."

And she didn't sound like she was just quotin'.

Wisteria paced back and forth in my bedroom, her orange high-tops squeaking on the hardwood flood every time she turned and headed in the opposite direction. She didn't say a word to me but just mumbled under her breath and pounded her fist into her palm, like she was playing short-stop in a baseball game.

Then all of a sudden she halted right in the middle of my bedroom and said, "Tell your mama you're gonna eat supper with me and sleep up at my house tonight."

"What's going on, Wisteria?"

"I'm not real sure, Bit. I just got me a hunch."

"What kind of hunch?"

"Just a hunch. No particular kind of hunch. We'll just have to wait and see."

And no matter how much I questioned her, that's all she'd say.

"Not sure about a thing, Bit. Just got a hunch. Don't want to jinx it by talking about it. And I just don't want to get your hopes up and then let you down. But I just got me this hunch."

* * *

Miss Faylene fixed us fried pork chops and candied yams for supper, which were real good, but I just wasn't in an eatin' mood. After supper I thanked Miss Faylene and told her how good her cooking was, and she thanked me for appreciating her efforts. Then me and Wisteria washed the dishes for her mama while she was overseeing Faye and Virginia's bath. Then we went out in the back yard to jump on the trampoline till it got dark.

Neither one of us felt much like jumping, so we lay down on the trampoline side-by-side and looked at the clouds while we talked.

"You okay?" Wisteria asked.

"Not real sure, Wisteria. A lot has happened lately."

It hadn't been but a few days since Palmer Lee had taken me up to his daddy's hunting lodge, and I was still mighty shook up. It didn't help that I couldn't tell my mama what had happened out of guilt and embarrassment, but I was hoping and praying that one day the whole thing would start to get fuzzy, like memories of your past do, and that, even if I could never forget it altogether, I might be able to tolerate it being a part of my life, like one of those learning experiences.

And on top of what Palmer Lee had done to me, somebody had gone and snatched Kitty. It dang near broke my heart.

"Come on in now, girls," Miss Faylene called from the kitchen door. "It's getting dark out there."

So we stood up and did one great big jump before we sprang off to the ground. We went inside and pulled out the sleeper sofa in Wisteria's living room and spread our sheets over it. Then we got out a light blanket and tossed it on top of the sheets. It was still warm during the day, but it was always right chilly at night up in the holler.

When I started getting my pajamas out of my bag, Wisteria whispered, "Don't put your pajamas on. Just stay in your clothes."

"But why?" I asked her.

"Just 'cause. Trust me, Bit," was all she'd say, still talking in her whispery voice.

The way Wisteria was acting was giving me the creeps, and I wasn't liking the way this was feeling at all.

"Does this have anything to do with your hunch?"

"Don't ask questions. I'll tell you later."

So I didn't ask any more questions, and we sat up on the sleeper sofa in our clothes, watching TV, waiting for Miss Faylene and Mr. Earl to go to bed.

When we heard Mr. Earl snoring something fierce, Wisteria scootched to the side of the sleeper-sofa, stood up, and said, "Let's go."

"Go where?"

"Shh, just follow me."

We slipped on our tennis shoes and jackets, and Wisteria whispered, "This way."

We tiptoed through the kitchen, where Wisteria grabbed the big flashlight that Miss Faylene kept on the shelf by the back door. She used it to scare off raccoons when they tried to get in the garbage can. Wisteria eased the back door open an inch at a time, careful not to let it creak, and we headed out into the back yard.

"Come this way," she said, scrunching down and tiptoeing toward the shed.

When we got there, Wisteria opened the door, and a sliver of moonlight cut through the pitch-black dark of the shed. I could see NaCl starting to hop around and click her little hooves, all excited, like we were coming to play with her.

"Here, hold the flashlight while I put NaCl in her pen," Wisteria said, shoving it in my hands. "And, whatever you do, don't turn it on."

When Wisteria had NaCl locked in her pen, bleating and kicking on the gate to get out, she came back to me and said, "Okay, close the door and sit down and get comfy. This could take all night."

Once the door was closed, I couldn't see a dang thing, so I felt around for Wisteria and eased myself down beside her and tried to get comfy, just like she'd told me to do.

"Now, tell me, Wisteria, what's going on?"

"Bit, me and you just might catch us a petnapper tonight."

"What makes you think we're going to do any such thing?"

"It's that hunch I was telling you about. You okay now?"

"Yeah, I guess so, but you're scaring me to death."

"Don't be scared," she said, patting my leg.

NaCl was making a racket, bleating all pitiful-like and tap dancing around in her pen, trying to get out to play with Wisteria, and I whispered, "Shouldn't she be quiet?"

Wisteria whispered back, "Nah, the more racket she makes, the better. She's our bait." Then she added, "And one more thing, no more talking."

So there we sat, me with Miss Faylene's raccoon flashlight, me and Wisteria not saying a word, by Wisteria's orders.

I'd have bet we sat there all quiet for hours and hours, but Wisteria swore it was only about forty-five minutes. But it was the longest, scariest forty-five minutes of my whole life.

Soon we heard a rustling outside the shed. My hands commenced to sweating and shaking, and my heart started beating all the way up in my ears. I was so scared.

My eyes had gotten used to the dark, and I could see Wisteria next to me, leaning back against the wall, looking all confident that she was gonna catch herself a petnapper.

Then we heard another sound outside. This sound was different from the sound of a fox or a squirrel or a raccoon. Footsteps. Human footsteps, not animal footsteps. It was pretty hard to hear over NaCl's ruckus, but they were definite human footsteps. They would come a little closer. And stop. Closer. Stop. Closer. Stop. It was scaring the puddin' out of me, and the closer the footsteps got, the harder my heart was beating, so hard I was sure I could hear it. I was scared whoever was walking around outside the shed could hear it too.

"Can you hear my heart pounding, Wisteria?"

"Heck, no! Now hush up and pay attention."

So I hushed up and held tight to the raccoon flashlight, hoping Wisteria was telling me the truth about not being able to hear my pounding heart, ready to take instructions from my best friend who had promised me she knew what she was doing.

Real easy-like Wisteria put her hand on my arm and whispered, "Not a sound, you hear? Don't care how scared you get, not a peep."

That was an awful lot to ask.

I heard the latch click and the door inch open, a slice of moonlight shining through the crack. As the crack got bigger and bigger, so did the slice of moonlight. Then I saw the figure of a person start to take shape in the light.

By now my heart was beating so hard it was hurting. I just wanted to be home in my own bed, home with my mama and my daddy and Buddy. But it was too late. I had to do what Wisteria told me to do and hope she was telling me the truth when she said she knew what she was talking about.

Leaving the shed door open, the figure stepped inside and tiptoed right past Wisteria and me, not three feet away. It was too dark to make out who it was, but I could tell it was a guy. My fear caught in my throat, and I made a little squeak. Wisteria reached over and grabbed my arm with one hand and put her other hand over my mouth. The guy stopped and swiveled his head side to side, probably trying to figure out where the squeak had come from. None of us moved. Then NaCl started making a racket, tap dancing in her stall. The figure let out his breath and moved toward Wisteria's little goat, probably confident that NaCl had made the squeaking noise.

The guy unlatched NaCl's stall and stepped inside. Then he picked up the little goat and cradled her in his arms, petting her and saying, "Sh, sh, sh."

Then he walked right back past us, holding that bleating goat, and disappeared through the door, leaving it open.

As soon as we lost sight of him, Wisteria took the flashlight from me and whispered, "Follow me, and don't make a sound."

We tiptoed from the shed just as the guy with Wisteria's goat disappeared around the side of the Joneses' respectable three-bedroom, one-and-one-half bath, brick ranch-style house. We followed his path, and when he reached the road, he turned left and headed up the holler in the direction of the old Mose Beemus property. We crept slowly and at a good distance, ducking behind trees when the petnapper would stop to shift NaCl's weight in his arms and give her a pat.

When we reached the top of the holler, the figure crept around the side of Senator Compton's hunting lodge and headed for the woods behind the property. Still we followed, me getting more terrified with every move, Wisteria showing amazing courage and confidence for a girl her age. We followed the petnapper into the woods a good distance, and the deeper we got in the tangled trees and vines and bushes, the more frightened I became. Just as I was about to tell Wisteria that I just couldn't go any deeper into the forest, she stopped dead in her tracks and flung her arm out for me to stop, as well.

Straight ahead was a clearing in the woods. The moon was full and shone through the trees to reveal a small shed of some kind, surrounded by a low fence with a gate. The ground was covered in moss and pine straw, and in the center of the clearing sat the petnapper, cradling NaCl in his arms, cooing to her. Beside him lay Kitty and Lord Poodle, resting his head on the guy's leg. Queen Elizabeth nuzzled his arm, while Larue and Miss Maudie's Rhode Island Reds strutted around in front of him. Chirp was sitting on his shoulder.

Wisteria motioned for me to follow her. By now I was certain everyone could hear my heart pounding, my teeth chattering in fear. But my brave friend continued to tiptoe quietly toward the clearing. When she got as close as she felt she could without being detected, she aimed the flashlight directly at the perpetrator. Then she turned on her high beam, revealing...Palmer Lee Compton.

He clung to NaCl and gathered the other animals to him. He looked small. He looked defeated. He didn't look like a well-bred, private-school-attending, rich purdy boy. He just hung his head as his shoulders shook.

Wisteria opened the gate to the clearing, and we stepped inside.

As we got closer, we could hear Palmer Lee sobbing and saying, "I'm sorry, just so sorry. I know I've hurt so many people, and I hope you can all forgive me."

I couldn't believe it, but I was embarrassed for him and actually felt sorry for him.

Wisteria and I sank to the ground in front of Palmer Lee, and I asked, "Why, Palmer Lee? Why did you do this?"

But he just kept on crying. So we waited. Finally, his crying slowed, and he raked his shirt sleeve across his snotty nose.

Then he said, "I just wanted somebody or something to love me, the way your mothers love you, the way you love each other."

"But what about your mama and daddy? They love you," Wisteria said.

"Really? They are so busy trying to get my father reelected, they don't even know I'm around."

"But what about all your friends in Raleigh?" I asked him.

"I haven't seen my friends all summer. You know why? 'Cause I haven't left this place all summer. All those trips my parents made to Raleigh? I didn't go. I wasn't invited. I stayed right here. Spent most nights in that shed right there. With all of them," he said, spreading his arms to indicate all the animals he had taken.

"But, Palmer Lee, why did you take all of our animals?" I asked him. "Why didn't you just get a dog or a cat, or a lot of dogs and cats, of your own. Surely, your rich daddy could afford to get you all the pets you want."

"He won't let me have a dog. Or a cat. Or any pet."

"Why's that?" Wisteria asked.

"I've always loved animals, ever since I was a little kid. I want to be a veterinarian. I want to go to the vet school at NC State. But my father won't allow it. He insists I go to Carolina and become a lawyer, just like him. But I've told him that I'm not going to go to Carolina, not going to be a lawyer. And since I've defied him by refusing to follow in his footsteps, he's punishing me by refusing to let me have a pet, and by keeping me away from my friends, making me stay up here by myself all summer."

"So you just decided to steal everybody's pets," Wisteria said, sarcastically.

"Guess so," Palmer Lee said, defeated. "Like I said, I'm so, so sorry. I'd planned to give them back before school started, but I just haven't figured out how to do it. And I hated the idea of parting with them. They've been my friends, my family all summer."

"Well, damn, Palmer Lee," Wisteria said, "I really wanted to hate you, but you make it so hard."

Palmer Lee sorta chuckled nervously and wiped his eyes with the tail of his shirt.

"But now I don't know what to do," he said. "I've really screwed up."

"That you have, but give me a minute to see if I can get you out of this mess," Wisteria told him.

Then she got real quiet, and I could see the wheels churning in that wise-beyond-its-years head of hers.

Finally she said, "Come on, Purdy Boy. Me and Bit here are gonna help you undo your crime. We've got about six hours to get all this livestock back to their rightful owners and get back to bed before we get caught. So we need to get a move on."

Wisteria stood up, leaned over, and took NaCl out of Palmer Lee's arms, saying, "I'm going to take NaCl, Kitty, and Larue home. You two take the rest of this menagerie and head on down to town."

Palmer Lee stood up, squeezed Wisteria's shoulder, and said, "Thank you, Wisteria. I owe you."

"Damn right you do, Purdy Boy.

"Now, Bit, if you get back to my house before I do, sneak in the back door and head for the sleeper sofa. And if Mama or Daddy hears you scratching around and comes checking on you, just get under the covers and pretend you're asleep."

"Got it," I said.

Palmer Lee and I filled our arms with animals and headed to town, shuttling them back to their rightful owners. Nobody locks up their houses in Lovington, so we cracked doors and slid pets right on in. The Rhode Island Reds were easy. We just dropped them off at their pens.

And all the while we were returning animals, Palmer Lee apologized, saying, "I'm so sorry, Bit. I didn't mean to hurt you."

"But why, Palmer Lee? You've explained stealing the animals, but why did you hurt me?"

"All the guys tease me..."

"About what?" I asked.

"They call me a fag because I've never been with a girl, never really had a girlfriend."

"Well, Palmer Lee, if you want a girlfriend, you're going about it all wrong."

"Yeah, I know that now," he said and hung his head.

At four in the morning, after we had dropped Queen Elizabeth at Miss Eulalee's B&B, Palmer Lee and I headed back up the holler.

When we reached Wisteria's house, all I said was "Bye, Palmer Lee," because that's about all I had left to say.

But he looked at me with the saddest eyes I'd ever seen and said, "I didn't mean what I said about you, Bit. I was just hurt and scared and embarrassed. You're about the nicest person I've ever met, much nicer than all my friends in Raleigh. They act privileged, like the world owes them something. You're just not like that, not at all. Thank you for being my friend this summer. I'm just sorry I didn't appreciate your friendship."

Then I watched him turn and trudge on up the holler road to his new, spacious, beautiful hunting lodge with a huge swimming pool, tennis court, and a rifle range. It should have been enough to make anyone happy. It should have. But Palmer Lee Compton didn't want things. He just wanted someone or something to love and to love him back. I was still hurt by what he'd done to me, but I hoped he could find what he wanted.

I sneaked in the back door of Wisteria's house and tiptoed across the kitchen to the living room. There I found Wisteria sitting up on the sleeper sofa, waiting for me.

"Dang, you're slow," she said.

"Guess it's 'cause I don't have any orange high-tops to make me run fast."

"Yeah, guess that's the reason."

"How'd you know, Wisteria?" I whispered, as soon as I'd crawled under the covers.

"Well, Bit, it hit me right 'tween the eyes when Sheriff Roudebush said that it all commenced when the tourists started coming into Miss Brenda's quilt shop."

"Right, but how did you come up with Palmer Lee?"

"Bit, each petnapping had the same M.O., so I figured the same person must have taken all the animals. And if it was somebody just visiting, it had to be someone who was visiting for a real long time. And most people just come for a day or a weekend. Except one person."

"Palmer Lee Compton."

"Bingo!"

"What really convinced me that it was Palmer Lee was when Kitty went missing. Purdy Boy had had plenty of opportunity to take your dog, but he didn't as long as you were sweet on him. It wasn't till you told him to leave you alone down at the Fall Is Just Around the Corner Festival that he sneaked onto your back porch and took Kitty. And since I'd made him good and mad, I figured it was just a matter of time before he came for NaCl."

"Wisteria, you're so smart."

"Damn straight, I am! Now, go to sleep. That purdy boy has been a thorn in my side all summer, and I need me some rest."

* * *

"It's a miracle!"

That's what most everybody said when all the Lovington animals showed back up in their own homes, all on the same night, safe and sound. And as much as Sheriff Roudebush would have liked taking credit for cracking the case, he couldn't explain their reappearance any better than he could explain their disappearance. The rightful owners didn't care, though. They were just happy to have their beloved pets back.

Palmer Lee went on back to Raleigh, and Wisteria and I made a pact never to divulge anything that had happened that summer. And just as we've abided by our friendship contract, we haven't broken our pact of silence.

TWENTY-THREE

The Summer
the Air Changed

Wisteria and I were sitting on the dock.

School had been back in for about three weeks, but it was still summer-hot during the day in Lovington. To keep cool I had my feet dangling in the water. Our jobs down at The Quilt Shop had ended when we started back to school, since that was our deal when Mama and Miss Nelda hired us.

Since I was in the tenth grade, I'd been moved up to Lovington High School on the third floor, but Wisteria was still in Lovington Middle School on the middle floor. She was just as smart as anybody in my class and could have done all the lessons, but I guess they figured they couldn't skip her ahead another grade. She'd already been skipped once. Mama said she was intellectually mature enough for high school but that she wasn't socially mature enough. Ha! Mama didn't know Wisteria like I did.

And it was best we kept it that way.

Since Wisteria and I didn't get to see each other all day long, we made the most of our time together after school and on weekends. Except Sundays, of course.

So one Saturday while we were sitting in the sun on the dock, I said, "I still can't believe you solved that crime, Wisteria. You're so smart."

"True, true. But it was just a matter of closely examining all the facts. You could have solved it, too, if you hadn't been so personally involved with the perpetrator."

"But I didn't. You did. Like I said, you're so smart."

"You know, Bit, sometimes my brain is my burden, but this time me being smart really paid off."

Then she just smiled kind of far away-like and started concentrating on her scab.

"This has been one crazy summer, hasn't it, Wisteria?"

"You got that right. Nothing's the same since Bug Jeter seen Jesus in that rock."

"Sad thing is, Jesus isn't even there anymore. Rain just washed him away till he's nothing more than a blur."

"Yeah," Wisteria said, "but if it hadn't been for Bug's Jesus rock, we'd still be little old Lovington, North Carolina that nobody had ever heard of. That Jesus rock changed everything. You know, I was thinking that even the air feels different, like it's all full of electricity or something. It's scary and fun and exciting and colorful and confusing all at the same time."

"Yeah, interesting way of looking at it."

Then Wisteria got real quiet and started concentrating hard on her scab, making me know she was thinking real deep about something. So while she was thinking deep, I watched a dragon fly skitter across the water right in front of us. Its body was iridescent green, and its black wings looked like a boat's rudders. I watched it skim around on the top of the water until its rudder-wings started vibrating real fast, so fast they were just a blur, and it took off and disappeared into a stand of trees.

"Something else real big has changed."

"What's that?"

"Daddy Earl's gotta leave," Wisteria said, still not looking my way.

"Why's that?"

"Guess Mama's fed up with him being up to no good. We moved up here so Papa Luke could keep an eye on him, but that hasn't worked out too good. Mama says maybe Papa Luke's just gotten too old and doesn't have it in him any more to keep his young'un in line."

"Where will Mr. Earl go?"

"Maybe he'll take a room over to the new Comfort Inn by the bypass. Or I'm thinking he may go on back and set up house in Papa Luke's rickety little trailer down by the river. Maybe not, though, since Mama seems to think that's where all the being up to no good has been happening since our family vacated the rickety little trailer and moved into our new respectable three-bedroom, one-and-one-half bath, brick ranch-style home."

By now the tears were streaming down Wisteria's face, dripping off her chin. She didn't even try to stop them. She didn't even call herself a damn sissy. Maybe she finally believed what I'd told her about bleeding the sorrow out, and she was giving it a try.

Wisteria was smart as a whip. She was so smart she could skip a grade. She was so smart she could figure out how to get a job long before she was old enough to even get a work permit. She was so smart she could solve crimes. She was so smart she could teach her older friend about boys. But her smarts couldn't make her change the one thing she wanted to change more than anything else in the world. So I just let her bleed her sorrow out, figuring she needed this time to be sad because she just wasn't smart enough to keep her Daddy Earl from being up to no good.

It seemed awful late in the season for mosquitoes, but one lit on my leg and bit the tarnation out of me. I whacked it, and it splatted, making a little star of my blood all around it. I spit on my finger and cleaned it off. Then I scraped the dead mosquito and my blood off my finger on the end of a dock board that was beginning to curl up from the summer heat and sun.

I noticed Wisteria's sorrow bleeding had stopped for the time being, and she had dried her face on the bottom of her tee shirt.

"Yep, everything has changed," I said, while I scratched the mosquito bite on my leg and Wisteria picked at the scab on her knee.

Then all of a sudden Wisteria yanked up her tee shirt and screamed, "I almost forgot! Looky here!"

There, on her chest, were two little pointed, pink boobs about the size of my mosquito bite.

"Well, where in the heck did those come from?"

"Damn if I know. I just got up this morning, and there they were."

"Gonna get you a boyfriend?"

"You know damn well I don't need any boobs to get me a boyfriend. I got my brain."

"I know that, Wisteria."

"But see there," she said, pointing to her new boobs, "*everything has changed.*"

I laughed at her and said, "Yeah, everything." Then I thought about it a minute or so and said to her, "No, Wisteria, come to think of it, there's one very important thing that hasn't changed, hasn't changed at all."

"What's that?" asked Wisteria, smoothing her tee shirt back down and looking at the little bumps her new boobs were making in the fabric.

I spit on my hand and smiled at her.

Nodding knowingly, Wisteria spit on her hand and smiled back, big enough to show me the gap in her front teeth.

We slapped our palms together and screamed loud enough for our voices to echo over the water and down the mountain ridge, "Best friends! Forever! ...ever! ...ever! ...ever!"

Then we jumped up, grabbed hands, and leapt, fully clothed, into the pond.

The End...

Till Something
Else Exciting
Happens

Acknowledgments

She came to us, fresh out of college, our last semester of high school. She was eager to teach us to write. We were eager to leave high school. She won. She showed us that our writing was not just an assignment, but an extension of who we were. She refused to settle for less than our best, and instilled that lesson in all of us. She taught us to love the written word and turned us into grammar nerds...who still laugh at the silliest of grammar jokes. Decades later her students still call her the best teacher ever. Thank you, Joyce Waddell, for refusing to let us settle for anything less than our best. And thank you for making me want to become a writer.

My sincere thanks to phenomenal authors Tracie Barton-Barrett, Heather Cobham Brewer, Michelle Garren Flye, and Leslie Tall Manning for their friendship, their encouragement, and their guidance through the chaos of 2020 and beyond. Writing can be challenging in the best of circumstances, but the year 2020 brought unexpected roadblocks, fears, angst, and discouragement. Without the support of these author-friends, *The Summer the Air Changed* may have never become a reality.

A writer friend once told me, "You need to meet Alice Osborn." Seven years ago I made a lunch date with Alice and found that my friend's advice was some of the best I've ever received. For seven years I've been a member and a two-time visiting author of Alice's book club, Wonderland. I am most grateful for Alice's friendship, her selflessness, and her genuineness. Thank you, Alice, for all you've been to me and for all you give to our writing community. We all love you.

It is so exciting when your novel finds a publisher, especially one you're certain is a perfect fit. Excitement and gratitude is what I felt when Janie Jessee from Jan-Carol Publishing wrote to say that she wanted to publish *The Summer the Air Changed*. So, thank you, Janie, for embracing my novel and for giving it a great home. And my sincere thanks, as well, to editor, Shanna Light, and communications director, Savannah Bailey, for their expertise in helping *The Summer the Air Changed* be the best it can be. And special thanks to the very talented designer Tara Sizemore, who understood my vision and created the perfect cover for *The Summer the Air Changed*.

Ed, we did it again. When we published *Getting the Important Things Right* in 2012, I couldn't have dreamed of releasing number six, *The Summer the Air Changed*, just nine years later. Yet, here we are. I, however, did the easy part—the writing—while you did all that behind-the-scenes stuff that I couldn't even imagine needed to be done. Thank you, Ed—my muse, my magician, my best friend.

I grew up in the wonderful small town of Covington, Virginia, in the Alleghany Highlands, nestled in the Shenandoah Valley. (Ed calls it Dick and Jane country.) If it weren't for my hometown, I wouldn't have known how to bring fictional Lovington, North Carolina to life. Had it not been for my childhood home, I wouldn't have known the squealing delight of swimming in a river fed by frigid mountain streams. I wouldn't have realized the joy of knowing everyone in town and everyone in town knowing me well enough to "tell my mother." I wouldn't have known the splendor of the Blue Ridge Mountains, had I not awakened to their glory each morning. And I certainly wouldn't have known the meaning of "up a holler." So, thank you, Covington, for nurturing me through my childhood and for helping me bring

Lovington to life. And thanks to all you Covingtonians, the most supportive friends and the best readers in all the world.

Bit Sizemore isn't just a character in *The Summer the Air Changed*. Bit and I began writing together in 2006, and she's always been by my side to share my anger, my fears, my uncertainty, my joy, my accomplishments. She calms me; she amuses me; she encourages me. Bit is my moral compass and everything I'd like to be: kind, loving, smart, talented, a good friend, a respectful daughter. Thank you, Bit, for being by my side for fifteen years. I'm confident that you and your best friend, Wisteria, are ready to be released to the wild. Fly free, but stay safe.

About the Author

Padgett Gerler grew up in the Appalachian Mountains of Virginia, where she loved small-town life, created lasting friendships, and swam in the icy, mountain-stream-fed Jackson River. Leaving the mountains for college, she graduated from North Carolina State University with an accounting degree. After earning her CPA certificate, she practiced accounting until, in 2010, she left her career to pursue fiction writing.

Padgett is the award-winning author of six published novels, her most recent (and her first Young Adult selection) being, *The Summer the Air Changed*. *Lessons I Learned from Nick Nack* and *Invisible Girl* were both awarded the indieBRAG Medallion, while *Lessons I Learned from Nick Nack* also received honorable mention in the 2014 Writer's Digest Self Published Book Awards. *The Gifts of Peican Isle* was a Finalist in the 2018 Best Book Awards sponsored by American Book Fest. Padgett's short story "The Art of Dying" won first place in the Southwest Manuscripters Awards. Her short story "I Know This Happened 'Cause Somebody Seen It" is featured in the anthology *Self-Rising Flowers*, published by Mountain Girl Press.

Follow Padgett on Facebook at Padgett Gerler, Author, twitter @mpgerler, and her website www.padgettgerler.com. Feel free to contact her at mpgerler@gmail.com.

Coming Soon

The Girl Who Feared Trains

When Tante was three, the flu pandemic of 1918 took her mama. She and big sister, Dixie, boarded the train for Savannah to live with their grandmother, Aunt Sissy, leaving Daddy back home in South Carolina. When, after seven years, Daddy remarried, Tante and Dixie left their beloved grandmother to return home, where The Great Depression and Daddy's tragic illness colored Tante's teen years. Train rides seemed to mean tragedy and loss for Tante, but, despite the heartache of separation and the uncertainty of what awaited at the end of each ride, she recalls a childhood of family who loved and nurtured her and the Real Mother who promised she'd never leave.

CPSIA information can be obtained
at www.ICGtesting.com
Printed in the USA
BVHW082058150222
629079BV00003BA/204

9 781954 978058